"Why the hell didn't you tell me?" Whit demanded.

"You weren't here," Drew reminded him. It still hurt to remember. Safe in his love, she had dared to dream for the first time in her life—foolish, foolish girl. She had built them a lovely castle in the sky, and when her prince had walked away, it had come crashing down all around her. After he had left her, she had found out she was pregnant. Day by day, challenge by challenge, she had survived. She would survive this day, this challenge, too.

"I wasn't here—but you knew how to find me. Why didn't you even try?"

Drew looked him in the eye. "Why didn't I?"

A spasm of emotion crossed Whit's face before his expression turned as hard as granite.

"Your secret's out now, Drew, and that changes everything...."

Dear Reader,

This month, Silhouette Romance is celebrating the classic love story. That intensely romantic, emotional and compelling novel you just can't resist. And leading our month of classic love stories is *Wife without a Past* by Elizabeth Harbison, a deeply felt tale of an amnesiac wife who doesn't recognize the FABULOUS FATHER she'd married....

Pregnant with His Child... by bestselling author Carla Cassidy will warm your heart as a man is reunited with the child he never knew existed—and the woman he never stopped loving. Next, our MEN! promotion continues, as Silhouette Romance proves a good man isn't hard to find in *The Stranger's Surprise* by Laura Anthony. In Patricia Thayer's moving love story, *The Cowboy's Convenient Bride,* a woman turns up at a Texas ranch with a very poignant secret. And in *Plain Jane Gets Her Man* by Robin Wells, you'll be delighted by the modern-day Cinderella who wins the man of her dreams. Finally, Lisa Kaye Laurel's wonderful miniseries, ROYAL WEDDINGS, continues with *The Prince's Baby.*

As the Thanksgiving holiday approaches, I'd like to give a special thanks to all of you, the readers, for making Silhouette Romance such a popular and beloved series of books. Enjoy November's titles!

Regards,

Melissa Senate
Senior Editor
Silhouette Books

Please address questions and book requests to:
Silhouette Reader Service
U.S.: 3010 Walden Ave., P.O. Box 1325, Buffalo, NY 14269
Canadian: P.O. Box 609, Fort Erie, Ont. L2A 5X3

THE PRINCE'S BABY

Lisa Kaye Laurel

Silhouette
R O M A N C E™
Published by Silhouette Books
America's Publisher of Contemporary Romance

Dedicated with love and pride to my Nana,
in tribute to her ninety-five years;
and in memory of my beloved Pop Pop,
whose gentle kindness lives on.

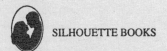 SILHOUETTE BOOKS

ISBN 0-373-19263-0

THE PRINCE'S BABY

Copyright © 1997 by Lisa Rizoli

This edition published by arrangement with Harlequin Books S.A.

® and TM are trademarks of Harlequin Books S.A., used under license.
Trademarks indicated with ® are registered in the United States Patent
and Trademark Office, the Canadian Trade Marks Office and in other
countries.

Printed in U.S.A.

Books by Lisa Kaye Laurel

Silhouette Romance

The Groom Maker #1107
Mommy for the Moment #1173
*The Prince's Bride #1251
*The Prince's Baby #1263

*Royal Weddings

LISA KAYE LAUREL

has worked in a number of fields, but says that nothing she's done compares to the challenges—and rewards—of being a full-time mom. Her extra energy is channeled into creating stories. She counts writing high on her list of blessings, which is topped by the love and support of her husband, her son, her daughter, her mother and her father.

Anders Point Gazette

IS THE PLAYBOY PRINCE A DADDY?
LOCAL SINGLE MOM'S SECRET IS OUT

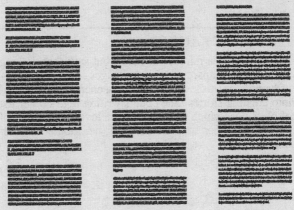

Chapter One

"She has her heart set on a fairy tale, but all the wishing in the world won't make it come true."

As the teacher's words sank in, Drew Davis felt a protest rise in her throat. "I don't—" she began, and then stopped herself. It was a rare and unwelcome mental lapse that had taken her back to a time when those words applied to *her*. Shaking it off, she looked around the first-grade classroom and then at the teacher. "Oh. You're talking about my daughter, aren't you?"

Mrs. Vittorini regarded her quizzically. "Of course I'm talking about Lexi. Why else would I have called you in for an emergency meeting?"

The urgent message on her office answering machine had struck fear in Drew's heart—blood-chilling, mind-numbing, parent fear. After rushing to school, she was relieved to learn that the emergency didn't involve broken bones or a quarantinable disease—but still, teachers didn't call parents in the middle of the school day with *good* news.

"I assume this has to do with Lexi's princess complex," Drew said.

"Yes. Frankly, I'm worried that she's taken it too far."

Drew had been afraid that would happen. She could think of no reason for her six-year-old daughter to think that she might be a real-life princess—yet Lexi was absolutely convinced that she was. For some time now her little girl had been living the part, acting out elaborate fairy-tale fantasies and always wearing some homemade crown or other. Telling herself that pretend play was an important part of childhood, Drew had given her daughter's fancies free rein and hoped the phase would soon pass.

The teacher went on. "The other day some of the children asked Lexi about her father, and do you know what she told them?"

Drew shook her head, while apprehension prickled along her scalp.

"She told them she didn't have a father, but she was going to have a prince."

"A...prince?"

Mrs. Vittorini nodded. "She made a 'magic lamp' at the craft table, and the class gathered around while she rubbed it, asking for a prince to appear. I got them all busy doing something else, but not before a few of them laughed at her."

Drew felt for her daughter. She herself had developed a tough veneer—that was what made her a survivor—but she had not passed that trait on to her sensitive daughter. Drew tried her best, but it still hurt to know that she couldn't always protect Lexi. "Thank you for being tuned in to her," she said.

"There's more. Yesterday she got into the art supplies and sprinkled glitter all over the room, saying that it was magic pixie dust that was going to make her prince appear."

"Oh, my gosh. I'm so sorry."

Mrs. Vittorini brushed the apology aside. "Messes happen. Lexi did the lion's share of the cleanup, believe me."

"Good. And if anything else happens—"

"It did."

Drew groaned inwardly. "What else?"

"On the playground this morning she tried to pull a prince out of Jason Greenwell's hat. This time she had the whole first grade laughing at her." The teacher's eyebrows puckered with concern. "And right before the children went in to the all-school nature assembly today, she announced to the class that her prince was definitely going to show up before the end of the day."

"Oh, no."

"Oh, yes. That's why I called you," Mrs. Vittorini said. "I just don't know what she's going to try next. Not to mention that her hopes are so high she's bound to come down with a crash by the end of the day. The assembly is going to end shortly and I thought that having you nearby—"

A burst of shouting and laughter from the gym brought Mrs. Vittorini to her feet. Her teacher's antennae were up. Without a word she headed down the hall toward the gym, with Drew right behind her.

The assembly had apparently gotten out of control. Looking through the gym door, Drew saw right away what all the laughter and shouting was about. And what she saw made her heart drop right into her toes.

In front of the crowded bleachers, under a banner that said Reptiles and Amphibians, were an assortment of cages and tanks filled with live specimens. And all alone at one of them stood Lexi, a smile on her face, a crown on her head and a frog in her hands. As Drew watched in dismay, her daughter bent down and gave the frog a kiss on the top of its head.

"There's no prince!" the children in the stands shouted.

"There will be!" Lexi shouted right back. She picked up another frog and gave that one a kiss, too.

"There's no prince!" The chant was louder this time, and the laughter in the stands grew, but Lexi determinedly reached for another frog.

"There will be!"

Drew stood rooted to the ground, both in awe of her daughter's guts and in dread of the inevitable humiliation Lexi would suffer after she kissed the last frog. Mrs. Vittorini rushed in to help the other teachers, who were in the stands trying to restore order, but to no avail.

Kiss.

"There's no prince!"

"There will be!"

Kiss.

"There's no prince!"

"There will be!"

A collective intake of breath was heard as Lexi picked up the last frog.

Kiss.

The stands fairly erupted with the shout, "There's no prince!"

Something inside Drew tore apart as she watched Lexi standing there, small and alone and with a handful of frog, unable to make her defiant reply this time. Drew started forward.

Suddenly a deep, commanding voice cut across the shrieks of laughter that filled the big room.

"Yes...there...is."

Silence fell. Drew watched in disbelief as a man strode from behind one of the big tanks to stand before Lexi. He was the last person she ever expected to see. But here he was—back in Anders Point after all these years. She froze, unable to do anything but stare, an old but familiar ache slicing through her.

In his jeans and leather jacket, he looked more like a bad-boy rebel than a fairy-tale prince, but there wasn't a woman in the world who wouldn't recognize the Prince of Hearts on sight, and Drew could tell by their murmurs of astonishment that the teachers in the audience were no exception.

His face perfectly serious, he bowed to Lexi. "I am Prince Whit of Isle Anders," he said.

Drew closed her gaping mouth and tried to get a grip on the emotions that churned inside her. Surprise at seeing Whit was quickly supplanted by dread, as she watched the prince kneel before Lexi, studying the little girl's delighted features.

Incredibly, Whit stood and looked at the audience, then, right at Drew. Her heart stopped in mid-beat as their glances caught and held for an electrifying moment; it was almost a physical connection. She stood motionless, helpless to break the contact.

Then Whit returned his gaze to Lexi, who looked up at him, enthralled.

"I am here at your wish," he said to her.

Whit spoke with the barest trace of an accent. His father was the ruler of Isle Anders, a small island not far from Iceland, but his mother had been born right here in Anders Point, Maine, and Whit had gone to college in the States. But there was a richness to his deep tones, a thrumming vibrancy that suggested the faraway, the exotic, the forbidden.

No one knew that better than Drew, who had been the first of many women to fall victim to Whit's powerful masculine lure. His having been born a prince was a quirk of fate, and his good looks were a gift from his parents' gene pool; but his reputation as the Prince of Hearts he had earned by his own willful actions.

And if she'd been the first to fall, she'd also been the first to break free, she reminded herself pointedly.

She had seen him for the first time in seven years just a few weeks ago, at the marriage of her friend Julie to his brother, Prince Erik. Among the guests, it had been easy to keep her distance from him, during those few hours. Other than that, she hadn't been this close to Whit since the summer she had fallen so deeply in love with him that she'd thought she wouldn't be able to draw breath without him by her side.

Now she saw that the passing of time had only served to enhance his appeal. He was, as all media accounts made him out to be, an extraordinarily handsome man. A handsome prince, no less; complete with stunning blue eyes, black hair that fell to his shoulders in luxuriant waves and the kind of body that looked scrumptious in everything from tuxedos to gym shorts. And then there was his legendary smile, the one he was right now beaming at her daughter, who stood looking up at him, spellbound, holding a papier mâché crown on the top of her head.

The daughter who meant the world to her. The daughter she would protect to her dying breath.

Lexi. Fear tightened every muscle in Drew's body until she ached with tension. She couldn't let him find out about Lexi. She had to hide her daughter from him. No matter what.

But there they stood, face-to-face. The tension became almost unbearable for Drew. She had to fight the impulse to run up front and snatch Lexi away, out of his sight; instead, she took a deep breath and tried to relax enough to allow rationality to regain a toehold. Of course Whit wouldn't suspect anything about Lexi, she told herself firmly. He had seen her at the wedding, and hadn't. There was no reason he would now, either. Drew herself was the only one who knew the truth—and she would *never* tell him.

Lexi found her tongue at last. "I am Princess Lexi of the first grade," she said proudly, dropping a curtsy. And then she smiled at him, her bewitching, little-girl smile. It revealed the gap where her two bottom teeth were missing. It revealed the dimple in her left cheek. And, in some intangible, inexplicable way, it revealed the secret that had weighed heavily on Drew's heart for seven long years.

Drew knew it had as she watched Whit's smile slowly fade. She squeezed her eyes shut, but when she opened them, the scene was still before her, the excited whispers of the crowd still flowing around her.

"I am at your service, princess," Whit said formally.

"Thank you, Your Highness," Lexi said gravely.

She conjured up her best royal vocabulary for the occasion. "When I require your services again, I shall not hesitate to summon you."

The prince bowed to Lexi once more. "Then I will bid you good-day." As abruptly as he had materialized, he disappeared, but not before looking out into the audience again. This time he skewered Drew with a sharp, questioning glance that boded ill.

The lunch bell rang, and teachers began lining up their classes at the gym door. Everyone was still buzzing about the fact that Lexi had conjured up a real prince, and Drew saw that the smile was still on her daughter's face as she got in line. Mrs. Vittorini reappeared at Drew's side.

"I thought she was doomed to disappointment," the teacher said to Drew, still breathless with the excitement of the royal visit. "But it looks like your little girl got her happy ending after all. I only wish the prince would have stuck around to fill us in on how she managed it." She sighed dreamily. "Oh well, I guess you can go now. I'm sure Lexi will be fine. As for the rest of us women—" She paused, her eyes twinkling.

As she studied Mrs. Vittorini's flushed face, Drew realized she wasn't the only one who'd been affected by the prince's startling appearance at the school. "I can't tell you how much I appreciate your concern for Lexi," she said, not wanting to speculate with the teacher about the reasons for Whit's visit. "I apologize for the disruptions she's been causing. I assure you, that behavior is going to stop."

"Don't be too hard on her. She's going through a rough patch, as we all do from time to time." Mrs. Vittorini smiled. "But she's a bright young lady with a wonderful imagination. Give her lots of support, and she'll sort things out on her own. Lexi will do just fine in this world.''

''I just hope I survive to see it,'' Drew said, managing a weak smile. ''Sometimes being a mom makes my job as sheriff seem like a stroll on the beach.''

Mrs. Vittorini laughed. ''No one ever said parenting was easy. Especially not me. I've got three teenagers.''

And nineteen six-year-olds, Drew thought as she watched her lead a ragged line of jumping, talking, laughing first-graders out of the gym.

Drew made a quick exit herself. It was chickening out, she knew, but she wasn't ready to face Whit just yet. And though she was curious herself about how he'd known of Lexi's dilemma, she didn't like that look he had given her. The last thing she wanted was to run into him now.

She did run into Whit, though. Literally barreled right into him as she left the school building.

He seemed to have been expecting it. He never budged an inch, just propped his hands on his hips and stared down at her.

''That was your daughter,'' he said in a dangerously low voice. It wasn't a question.

Drew didn't shrink from his gaze. ''Yes. Thanks for what you did in there. She—well, she got herself into a tight spot, and if you hadn't—''

''Forget it,'' he said roughly, cutting her off.

''Well, then... goodbye,'' Drew finished breathlessly, eager to get away.

She turned to leave, but the sound of Whit's voice, low and vibrating with warning, stopped her. ''It's time you and I had a little talk, Drew.''

All of Drew's instincts warned her to go on the defense. "Sorry to refuse your gracious request, Your Highness, but I don't have time to chat," she told him, forcing a light tone. "Some people in this world have to work for a living, and I am one of them. So you'll have to excuse me. It's late, and I've got to get back to my office."

"Your office be damned. You're coming with me." He led her down the front walk toward where a limousine was parked.

She planted her feet. "I'm not going anywhere."

"Fine. Then we can have it out right here on the sidewalk."

From the look on his face, Drew knew that he meant it. She glanced at the school building with its row of windows facing in their direction. One of those rooms was Lexi's classroom.

"All right," she said shortly, giving in. "Since I have no alternative."

The driver started to get out of the limo, but Whit waved him off and held the back door open for Drew himself. She refused to look at him then, or during the drive, which lasted no more than a minute. Whit had the driver pull into a turnoff for a scenic overlook of the ocean. No one else was there.

As soon as the limo rolled to a stop, Drew opened the door herself and scrambled out of the back seat. She waited while Whit followed, his movements slow and deliberate.

Drew faced him defiantly, knowing that she had to make the most of her anger, because it was the only thing holding her together right now.

"What did you want to talk about, Your Highness, that you had to practically kidnap me?" she asked, her voice sounding far more in control than her insides felt. Her heart was pounding so hard it drowned out the sound of the surf crashing onto the rocks below.

His jaw looked like it was carved out of granite. "You owe me an answer, Drew."

"What answer?" she asked, crossing her arms to stop them from shaking.

"Let's not play games, here. This is damned well as important to you as it is to me."

Drew hitched her trembling chin higher and forced herself to keep looking right at him, her silence warning him to go on only if he dared.

He did dare. His blue eyes were cold as the icy waters surrounding his North Atlantic homeland as he fixed a stare on her.

"So tell me. Tell me how a little girl kissing frogs in Maine could bear such a striking resemblance to a portrait of a child that hangs in my father's castle on Isle Anders." His voice was low, strained. "My portrait, Drew."

Chapter Two

The moment Drew had been dreading for years had arrived at last, and it was far worse than she had feared.

All of her maternal instincts screamed at her to protect Lexi at any cost. Warring with them was her conscience, which protested that, no matter what the consequences, Whit had a right to know the truth.

Her inner battle raged until she heard Whit speak again. This time his voice was rough with emotion.

"Drew, tell me. Is Lexi my daughter?"

The word that would change three people's lives forever came out as barely a whisper.

"Yes."

It had come down to no decision at all, for Drew. It was one thing not to have sought Whit out to tell him about Lexi. It would be something else entirely to stand there and answer his direct question with a lie.

She watched the reactions play across his face and

was relieved when he settled on anger. That gave her back the strength to face him.

"Why the hell didn't you *tell* me?" he demanded.

"You weren't here," she reminded him. It still hurt to remember. Safe in his love, she had dared to dream for the first time in her life—*foolish, foolish girl.* She had built them a lovely castle in the sky, and when her prince had walked away, it had come crashing down all around her. After he'd left her, she'd found out she was pregnant. Day by day, challenge by challenge, she had survived. She would survive this day, this challenge, too. Taking a deep breath, she returned Whit's stony stare.

"I had no reason to suspect you might be pregnant when I left," he said, his expression as hard as the rocky shoreline they stood above. "How did it happen, anyway?"

Drew raised one eyebrow eloquently.

"You know what I mean," he said, his voice warning that his patience was being stretched to its limits. "We always took precautions."

As the daughter of an unwed mother, who had left her to be raised by her grandmother, Drew had often vowed that the last thing she would ever do was repeat her mother's mistake. Whit had been her first lover—her only lover—and as hot as the lovemaking they'd shared that golden summer was, he had taken full responsibility for protecting her. She had seen that as yet another proof of his love; which only showed that a person could make two mistakes at the same time.

"No method is foolproof," she said. And there was no bigger fool in the world than she had been that summer. "We're not the only two people that this has ever happened to."

"That's right. It took *two* of us," he snapped. "Okay, I wasn't here—but you knew how to find me. Why didn't you even try?"

She looked him right in the eye. "Why didn't I?" she flung back.

He looked away then, but before he did, she thought she saw a spasm of emotion cross his face. For a moment she felt for him, automatically starting down a well-worn path of caring that had long been blocked off. Don't go that way, Drew, she warned herself. Let him sweat this out. Just let him! His silence told her that he must have some memory of the day he had shattered her dreams.

After a moment he swung his glance back to her; it was as hard as granite. "I still think you should have told me about the baby."

Like she hadn't thought about that, for endless hours. Her pride would keep *her* safe from him—she didn't need to learn a painful lesson twice—but the baby was another matter entirely. She'd had to decide which was worse for Lexi: no father at all, or a man who didn't want to be a father, who might up and leave again at any time, as he had left her. The rambling ways of the Prince of Hearts had been documented enough by the media over the ensuing years to make Drew sure she'd done the right thing.

"Well, I didn't," she said, looking up at him in defiance. "And if you hadn't figured it out on your own, I still wouldn't."

"Your secret's out now, Drew, and that changes everything," he said, his voice taut with warning.

Fear wrapped its icy fingers around Drew's throat.

"What do you mean?" she asked, unable to keep a note of desperation from creeping into her voice.

"You've played God for seven years, Drew. No more."

"But no one else knows, Whit—I swear! No one knows we were lovers, and I've never told anyone who Lexi's father is. I'll never expose you publicly or bring a suit against you or anything like that! If I'd wanted that, I would have done it long ago. Lexi and I are doing fine. Nothing has to change. We go our way, and you go yours."

Whit stared at her. "Do you expect me to just turn my back and forget I have a *daughter?*"

No. Even through her anger Drew could see that there was a world of difference between the nineteen-year-old who didn't want to be a family man and the grown man who'd just discovered he had a child of his own. But his feelings weren't her concern. Lexi was. She looked up at him. "Whit, please. For Lexi's sake, don't do anything about this."

He set his jaw and said tightly, "I am most definitely going to do something."

Determination to protect her daughter gave Drew a backbone of steel. "Just what are you going to do, Your Highness?" she demanded, hands on hips.

"How the hell do I know?" he shot back. "But I'll think of something, with or without your cooperation."

Drew didn't feel like cooperating! What she felt like doing was belting him. "My first choice is for you to leave, just like you did seven years ago. But since you seem determined to be difficult about this, you had better believe that I will darn well have a major say in how this affects my daughter," she said.

She lowered her voice and added, "All I care about is what's best for Lexi."

Whit's flare of anger seemed to be spent. "You might not believe it, but so do I," he said feelingly. "We need to figure this out, together."

Drew took a step backward, holding up her hands. "Look, Whit, I can't talk about this now. I have to get to work." What she really needed was to get away from him, to think.

"All right," he conceded. "Tonight. I'll come to your house."

"No!" She almost shouted it.

The line of his mouth was grim. "At the castle, then. Can you get someone to watch Lexi?"

"Yes," said Drew, unable to keep the disappointment of defeat out of her voice. "I'll be there at eight."

After the limo dropped Drew off at her car in the school parking lot, Whit ordered the driver to go back home. It sounded funny to say that. He was a citizen of the world, as the saying went, and he'd always had more roam than home in him. But for the foreseeable future, he would be living right here in Maine, in the castle at the tip of Anders Point that had been owned by his family for years. Not that it was his decision to be stuck on this finger of land on the Maine coast. He was here on his father's orders.

He sat back in the seat, and a crackling sound reminded him of the crumpled piece of paper that nestled in his pocket. Finding it stuck in the big iron gate when he'd arrived at the castle had not only sent him to the school, it had sent his life into turmoil. His thoughts turned to the beautiful little girl he'd met today—*his* little girl. A lump thickened in his throat as he remembered her features—so very like his own. How could Drew have kept his daughter from him?

"Phone call for you, Your Highness," the driver said, interrupting Whit's chaotic thoughts.

It was Whit's father. "I wanted to see how you were doing since you left Isle Anders," King Ivar said.

"You mean, since you sent me away," Whit clarified. For the past months, following his father's heart surgery, Whit had been shouldering the major responsibility for ruling the kingdom. But now King Ivar's recovery was complete and Whit's older brother, Prince Erik, had returned from his honeymoon with his bride, Julie. The king decided that Erik, his elder son and heir to the throne, should resume his former duties. And he wanted Whit to move on to the next in a long string of different jobs he had given him.

"Yes. Since I sent you to Anders Point," the king agreed.

Whit had learned long ago that he couldn't argue with his father's reasoning where his ever-changing assignments were concerned. And right now, he had more important things on his mind than his next royal duty, not that he was going to discuss those things with his father. Telling the king about Lexi would only confirm his father's feeling that his second son knew nothing of duty and responsibility. "Have you decided what you want me to do?" he asked.

"What would you like to do?"

Whit held his hand over the mouthpiece and swore. He was in no mood to play games. "Your Majesty,

I stand ready to perform whatever duty you assign me," he said. "As usual."

The king was silent for a moment, as if thinking. "I have been considering giving you some time off."

"Time off? Why?"

"I had a hiatus during my surgery, Erik had a honeymoon. Why shouldn't you take a little vacation, too?"

"I don't need a vacation, Your Majesty." What he needed was his usual fast-paced life-style—fast enough to use up some of his boundless energy, too fast to allow any introspection. "What would you like me to do while I'm here?"

The king paused, as if choosing his words carefully. "Just do what comes naturally," he said.

"As a *prince?*" Whit gave a derisive laugh. That was one thing that didn't come naturally to him, as his father very well knew. One of his botch-ups had nearly made the whole country grind to a halt. Whit wasn't like his father, or even like his responsible older brother. From the get-go he was the sort who colored outside of the lines, not a prime qualification for a role that's heavy on tradition. Whit was a prince by birth, a rebel by trade, and he'd walked an uneasy line his whole life—never disobeying a royal command, but never living up to his father's expectations either.

"Do what needs doing, my son, and trust that all things unfold in the fullness of time," the king said, unperturbed.

"As you wish, Your Majesty," Whit said, swearing again as he hung up the phone. His father loved to talk like that, and it drove him crazy.

The limo bumped up the gravel road that led to the

castle, stopping at the iron gate, which this time had no ragged piece of paper stuck in it. A lifetime had gone by since he'd found that note, which at a cursory glance he'd been ready to tear up. Then at second glance he saw that it wasn't written in red lipstick, but red crayon. This wasn't the usual tawdry proposition, but a missive with words of hope and longing written in a child's unschooled hand.

His child's, he now knew. Was that why it had beckoned him, so irresistibly, to the school?

After opening the gate, the driver pulled the limo up to the steps leading to the front door.

"Which room would you like your bags in, Your Highness?" he asked.

"I don't care," Whit said.

"The north suite has a lovely view this time of—"

"Fine, fine. Whatever."

"After that, is there anything else you'd like me to—"

"Yes," said Whit. "Get lost."

The young man stared at him. "Excuse me?"

"You heard me, Sloane. Get lost."

Sloane blinked. "Do you mean permanently? When your father hired me, he told me my services would be needed at least until the end of the year."

Whit looked at him. He was young—about nineteen, the age when young men make stupid, selfish mistakes. He was also handsome, cocky and, it seemed, chatty—all of which Whit found unspeakably irritating right now. "What's your real name, kid?"

"Sloane."

Whit glared at him.

"Okay, that's my last name. It's Gary Sloane, but

Gary didn't sound right for a chauffeur," the young man said amiably, adding, as an afterthought, "Your Highness."

"How old are you?"

"Nineteen."

Bingo. "Listen, Sloane," Whit said. "When I want to fire you, I'll say, 'You're fired.' When I want you to get lost, I'll say, 'Get lost.' Do you see the difference?"

"Yes, Your Highness. Absolutely."

"Good." Whit took the steps two at a time and yanked open the front door.

"Your Highness." Sloane's voice from behind stopped him.

Whit turned back around. "Aren't you lost yet, Sloane?"

"Yes. No. I mean, almost. But I wanted to know how long you want me to stay lost for."

"Until tomorrow morning."

Sloane was taken aback. "But, Your Highness, I live here at the castle. The king hired me to be the caretaker, too, since Julie used to do that before Prince Erik married her and—"

Whit held up his hand. "Do you have somewhere else to stay?"

Sloane's youthful brow frowned in thought. "Well, I suppose I could stay at my sister's. She's—"

"Good. Do it. Get lost until tomorrow morning."

"Yes, Your Highness."

"Oh, and Sloane?"

"Yes?"

"Where I go, what I do and with whom I speak are my own business. Not yours or your sister's or anyone else's. Is that clear?"

"Like crystal, Your Highness," Sloane said, and gave him a snappy salute.

With a groan, Whit went into the castle and slammed the heavy wooden door shut behind him.

Luckily no emergency calls came into the sheriff's office the rest of the afternoon, because Drew could do nothing but worry about what had happened.

Whit knew. He *knew*.

Her fears tormented her. What if he tried to take Lexi away from her? He was rich and powerful. Surely, if it came down to any battle between them, he would win easily. How could she live without Lexi?

The thought was too horrible to contemplate. Whit wouldn't, *couldn't*, do that to her—to them. Anyway, it made no sense for a playboy like him to want a child around, cramping his style. Her worries on that front subsided, only to be replaced by more realistic, and therefore, more haunting, ones.

Lexi was very needy right now. And no one would fit the bill for what she needed—at least, on the surface—except Whit. First of all, he was charming. No female, no matter how old or young, was immune to that charm. Second, he had rescued her. The look of worshipful gratitude on her face had reached Drew way in the back of the gym. But most of all, he was a *prince*. Of course Lexi would love him!

But where would that leave her daughter? Drew wondered. In the same place Whit had left her—all alone with the shattered fragments of her beautiful dreams?

* * *

Whit spent the afternoon pacing for miles along the stone-walled corridors of the castle.

He had been totally and completely thrown by the news he'd gotten that day. He had a daughter. A *daughter!*

The unexpectedness of it had sent him into turmoil, and the color of his reaction was as ever-changing as a kaleidoscope. He would pace by the refrigerator and get an inexplicable urge to pop open one of the champagne bottles left from Erik and Julie's wedding. Then he'd pace into his father's library and want a shot of something stronger from the liquor cabinet to fortify his jangling nerves. When he passed a telephone, his fingers itched to dial his brother or his friend Prince Lucas for moral support. When he passed one of the windows that overlooked the town, he would stop and wonder what *his daughter* was doing. When he passed a mirror, he'd wonder what *he* was doing. When he passed the big clock, whose hands moved in slow motion, he'd wonder how he was going to last until eight o'clock, when Drew would come.

He'd never had any father fantasies. They were too far from reality for him, starting as they did with a minister saying, "You may kiss the bride," and gradually progressing to a doctor saying, "Congratulations, it's a—"

It was a girl. He felt a sudden, irrational guilt that he hadn't paid more attention to her the first time he had ever seen her, at Erik and Julie's wedding here at the Anders Point castle. But the littlest guest at the wedding had been rather preoccupied with his father, the king, charming him out of his crown with her beguiling smile.

And Whit had been preoccupied with Drew. That occasion had been the first time he had seen her in seven long years, and the power of the attraction he had always felt for her had hit him full force. And that was without even speaking to her, because Drew had pointedly avoided him. He himself was painfully aware of the memory of having broken her heart by leaving. So while he had respected her obvious wishes and steered clear of her, even from across the ballroom it had been impossible to keep his eyes off her.

Finding out that the little blond girl was her daughter had been a shock. He remembered feeling a stab of jealousy that Drew had replaced him so quickly. Well, why not? He had stepped aside and left her with the hope that she would find the kind of family man she was looking for—a marrying man, steady and responsible, whom she could depend on to stand by her and give her the children she wanted and the happiness she deserved. Then he'd discovered that there was no husband to complete the family picture.

The idea that this replacement lover had left Drew alone to raise his child had filled Whit with anger. It had never dawned on him that there was a chance that Drew's little girl might be his, because he had figured Lexi to be four or five at most. When she had announced this morning that she was in first grade, it had been his first hint at the truth. Then, when she had looked up at him, the resemblance he'd seen had told him the rest.

Drew's little girl didn't have a daddy because *he* was her daddy.

There would be no nine-month waiting period for Whit. Fatherhood had been thrust upon him. And he knew precious little about first-grade girls in general, and even less about his daughter in particular. Lexi had done six years of growing up without him, and already had her own set of likes and dislikes, quirks and charms, fears and strengths, none of which he knew anything about.

He thought about that, and decided it wasn't quite true. He knew she was fascinated by royalty; seemed to think, in fact, that she was a princess, without knowing that it was true. He knew she had her mother's courage and stubbornness, having seen her facing a crowd of dubious peers with nothing but the strength of her own conviction. He knew she was vulnerable, too. That was why he had come to her rescue, before he had even known she was his. Something more than the words in red crayon had spoken to him when he'd read that note.

Had she needed rescuing in the past, when he wasn't there to do it? Would he get to do it again, to feel that rush of protectiveness, to bask in the warmth of a gap-toothed smile that made him feel ten feet tall?

He didn't know. He didn't know where Drew would want to go with this; not only had she kept Lexi a secret from him all this time, but she had also made no secret of why. What's more, he didn't know where *he* wanted to go with this. It was too new to him, too foreign to his life, too earthshaking.

But from the first moment the discovery had rocked his world, one fact had remained unshaken, solid to the core. He had first put this immutable fact into words for Drew: he could not walk away and forget he had a daughter. Beyond that, everything else was still trembling from the aftershocks. If things ever fell into place, he might have a clue as to what he was going to do.

By late afternoon Whit was beginning to feel like a tiger in a cage. He had to go somewhere—anywhere. Grabbing his battered leather jacket, he slammed out of the castle and let habit take his feet around back, to the outbuilding.

The distant rumble of a motorcycle through her office window, a sound out of place in Anders Point, captured Drew's attention. Life in crisis or not, she was the sheriff; and although here in this small New England town that meant more paper pushing than outlaw chasing, she still would have to find out which local teenager had gotten himself a new toy and then lecture him about not launching himself off the edge of the bluff by taking a curve too fast.

And it could happen, Drew knew. When she was a teenager, she herself had ridden the curvy roads overlooking the ocean on the back of a motorcycle— Whit's motorcycle. Somehow she had survived those wild and carefree days.

These days, Drew had a hard time remembering she had ever been wild and carefree. Mature and responsible had been her style for the past six years, since Lexi had been born. If her job as the town's only elected official wasn't quite what she had aspired to once upon a time, at least it provided a steady income. If that income was just enough to get by on, at least her hours were flexible. If the demanding life of a single mother wasn't her fairy tale come true, the rewards of having Lexi made it all worthwhile. Luckily she had the help of her friend Annah, for moral support as much as for emergency baby-sitting. All in all, she was managing. She had hardly wasted time these busy years wishing for her prince to come back to her. Far from it. But like it or not, here he was.

She had to try her best to hang on to her disappointment and hurt, her down-to-earth realism and down-East practicality, because coming face-to-face with her past was too much to handle without them. Without them, she was very much afraid that the awareness she'd felt earlier, during that first unguarded moment when she'd looked at Whit, might spring up in their place.

And that would be a mistake she couldn't afford to make, for her sake and for Lexi's.

As it turned out, the prince was all that the kids talked about after school, as Drew stopped traffic for them during crossing guard duty. The younger ones were wide-eyed; the sixth-grade girls jabbered excitedly about how "cute" the prince was; even the boys decided that the whole thing had been "way cool."

From where Lexi sat on the curb, waiting, Drew could see her eyes shining. After she had taken the last group across, Drew went over and sat next to her.

"Mommy, did you hear what happened today?" Lexi asked.

"Actually, I saw it," Drew told her.

"You were there? You saw the prince appear, like magic?"

With a wistful smile, Drew pulled her little girl onto her lap and enfolded her in a hug. After a few minutes Lexi shifted restlessly, so Drew set her back on the curb.

"There was no magic," she said gently. "This is

real life, Lexi, not a fairy tale. And Whit Anders is a real man.''

"A real *prince*," Lexi said decidedly.

Drew clamped down on all the responses unfit for six-year-old ears. Instead she said, "Your teacher told me about your behavior over the past few days."

Lexi looked at her with big green eyes. "I know, and I'm sorry. It was just so important, Mommy."

"I trust that this won't happen again?"

"Oh, no," Lexi assured her happily. "Because now the prince finally came."

Ugh. Drew bit back her frustration and asked, "Lexi, why don't you tell me why the prince came to your school?"

Lexi's expression turned earnest. "Well, you see, I needed a prince. So I wrote a note to King Ivar."

No surprise. Lexi had taken a shine to the king at Erik and Julie's wedding. "You asked King Ivar for a prince?"

"Yes, in a note, and I put the note in the gate when we walked up the castle road to pick flowers. And a prince *did* come! I just knew he would, Mommy."

Drew sighed. "Lexi, why do you need a prince, anyway?" she asked.

"To be my champion, of course," Lexi said seriously.

"Your champion?"

"Like the knights that ladies have in stories. My prince will be like that."

Her prince. Her little girl didn't have a father, so she wanted a prince to champion her, someone strong and fearless to stand beside her and fight for her. Drew's heart ached. She took Lexi's hand, and they walked to the car and got in.

Drew pulled away from the school. "And you

think Whit is going to be your prince?'' she asked, fearing the inevitable.

To her relief, Lexi frowned. ''I don't know if he's the one yet. He has to prove himself. This is very important, you see.''

Remembering the stories they had read, Drew felt as if she was finally catching on. ''Lexi, are you going to test him, to see if he's worthy of being your prince?''

''Yes.''

Great. Since his appearance that morning, he was certainly off to a rousing start, in Lexi's eyes. Drew, who'd had her life so well ordered, had the feeling that parts of it were breaking off and spinning out beyond her reach. Hanging on to part of it that wasn't—the need for food—she parked the car. ''Here we are at McCreedy's.''

They walked up to the small, family-owned grocery store that served Anders Point. Lexi went first, as usual, jumping on the black rubber mat at the entrance.

''Open...in the name of Princess Lexi,'' she commanded, pointing at the door. When it did, she giggled and called for Drew to catch up.

Drew did, and after they went in she turned and pointed back at the door. ''Close...in the name of the law,'' she said. It did, Lexi giggled, and Drew wondered how many such simple, comfortable rituals in their everyday life together were about to be destroyed.

Whit had found his old motorcycle where he'd left it in a corner of the outbuilding seven years ago, the last time he'd been at the Point for any length of time. After giving it a cursory tune-up and fill-up, he had slung his leg over the leather seat and taken off, faster than he knew he should, down the castle road, which curved its way to town along the bluff that dropped off straight into the Atlantic Ocean. But he could never go fast enough to outrun those old memories. There were reminders everywhere he looked.

The first house he'd passed was hers.

He'd known Drew almost all his life. When they were kids, they'd played together with Julie, during the summers that he spent on the Point. But that summer seven years ago, Julie hadn't been around, and he and Drew had had a secret romance. What they'd had was powerful, which was what had made it so damn scary. It was real love, Whit knew now, because it had been unselfish. She had wanted a dream, but he'd wanted what was best for her—and that wasn't a man like him, with his ponytail, motorcycle and crown that didn't seem to fit. Not wanting to fail her, he had left her.

After cruising the back roads most of the afternoon, he cut his speed as he entered the town, chugging along the quiet streets. A lot of road had disappeared under his wheels since he'd left town seven years ago. He wasn't proud of his footloose reputation, but he had always been sure he had done the right thing by leaving Drew.

Now he wasn't sure about anything.

He had just pulled into the only gas station in town when he heard a now-familiar voice.

"Look, Mommy! It's the prince!"

He looked at the little grocery store next door, and first met Drew's eyes, which went wide with dismay, before he saw Lexi. She was grinning up at him over a paper bag she hugged to the front of her while she stood on the sidewalk, her homemade crown still perched on her head.

An urge to sweep her into his arms made a sudden, sneak attack on him. Instead, he got off of his cycle and bowed to her as he had earlier. "Princess Lexi, would you do me the honor of allowing me to carry your bundle?"

Momentarily shy, she nodded and surrendered the grocery bag. Before Drew could protest, Whit took the bag she was carrying, too.

"Which way to the royal carriage?" he asked.

Lexi skipped ahead, pointing out a compact car that had seen better days, and lots of them. Whit felt a shaft of regret, thinking of all he could have provided for them, as Drew opened up the trunk.

Lexi had apparently found her voice, for she began peppering him with questions.

"Where did you come from?" she began.

He stowed the bags in the trunk. "I rode here on my motorcycle from the castle. That's where I'm staying, here at the Point."

She registered that information, then continued questioning. "But where did you come from in school this morning?"

"I found your note in the gate."

"But were you under a spell? Was my kiss magic? Did it turn you from a frog into a prince?"

Whit glanced at Drew, who was biting her lip. He went with his instincts.

"I was already a prince, so your kiss couldn't turn me into one," he told Lexi honestly. When her face fell, he couldn't help adding, "But I'll be darned if it didn't look like those frogs were smiling when you kissed them."

Lexi giggled, then abruptly asked him another question. "Are you a stranger?"

When he hesitated, Drew interrupted. "Lexi, it's time for us to go." She slammed the trunk closed.

"Could you wait a minute, please, Mommy? I just have to know this one thing," Lexi told her firmly, but not impolitely. "Are you?" she asked Whit again.

He thought about it. It was a complicated question, far more complicated than she could know. He *was* a stranger, yet he was bound to her by one of life's closest connections.

"Why do you want to know?" he finally asked her, hunkering down so that he was at eye level with her.

"Because if you're a stranger, I can't do something I really want to do."

"You'd better ask your mommy, princess."

Lexi lost no time in appealing to Drew. "Is he, Mommy?"

Whit watched a thousand shadows roll across the eyes of the woman he had once known so intimately, who was now a stranger to him.

At last she swallowed and said, "I've known Whit since I was your age. He's not a stranger."

That was all Lexi needed. She straightened her glitter-covered crown and, without hesitation, came up right beside him. He could smell the sweet fragrance of baby shampoo in her silky hair as she leaned toward him with a smile as innocent as youth, as wise as time. Then she planted her puckered lips on his cheek and left a tiny, damp kiss there.

She and her mother were gone before he straightened up from his crouch. No doubt Drew had seen how shaken he was.

Frogs aside, Lexi's kiss was indeed magic.

It had turned him into a father.

Chapter Three

Drew held on to Lexi a little too long that night when she hugged her at bedtime.

But all the clinging in the world wouldn't keep Lexi from being hurt, and it might let her daughter pick up on the fear that was flowing through her, cold as the ocean water outside. So Drew put on a determinedly cheerful smile as she said good-night and turned off the light.

She had to tell Annah, who was staying with Lexi, where she was going; but luckily her friend wasn't one to pry. Although Annah hadn't grown up on the Point, she knew that Drew and Whit had been friends since childhood, so she thought it natural that they would want to get together now that he was in town.

Drew decided that walking to the castle might calm her fears, and it did. More accurately, the crash of the waves and rush of the wind whipped up her courage. By the time she knocked on the front door of the

stone castle, she could have taken on the world with
her bare hands.

Whit took a long time answering, so she knocked
again, even more forcefully. A moment later the
heavy door swung open.

"Sorry," he said as he let her in. "I didn't hear
your car come up the drive."

"I walked. It's not far."

He looked at her for a moment. "I remember," he
said softly.

Drew looked away, momentarily thrown by his
words. She remembered, too. He had walked that
same walk many times himself, sometimes going the
other way in the middle of the night, hours after he
had secretly dropped her off at her grandmother's
house. Those nights he would stand outside her first-
floor bedroom, giving her slow, secret kisses through
the window, then running his lips along her ear as he
whispered that he hadn't been able to make it until
morning without the taste of her. His passion had
been intoxicating, and she had savored every drop of
it.

But memories of those nights had no bearing on
this one. Tonight Drew had to harden herself against
that one period of weakness in her past and get by on
grit, like she'd done ever since.

"Let's get started," she said briefly. "Annah's
baby-sitting for me, and mornings at her coffee shop
start early."

Whit nodded and led her through the front entry-
way. He was still wearing his jeans, the worn denim
clinging like a beautifully made second skin. To keep
her eyes off him as he walked along the stone floor
in front of her, Drew looked around her.

The castle had been built long ago by Whit's ancestors, and had been mostly used by the Anders family as a second home, convenient for official travel to the United States yet secluded for vacations. On occasion, Whit's father, King Ivar, had held charity balls there. Julie, besides being the castle's caretaker, had been in charge of planning the last one, a few months earlier. Because King Ivar had been in the hospital for heart surgery, Prince Erik had hosted the ball. That was the night he had announced his engagement to Julie.

But tonight the ballroom was dark and quiet as Drew walked past it. She followed Whit into a room she knew to be the king's library, declined his offer of a drink and sat down in a leather armchair opposite him. When she sank in too far, she got up and chose instead a straight-backed wooden chair which put her on eye level with Whit. She curled her fists around the ends of the armrests and faced him.

She took a breath and began, her voice strong. "You're going to have to—"

"Is Lexi in bed?" he asked softly, interrupting her.

She gave him a surprised look. "Yes. Eight o'clock is her bedtime."

He closed his eyes for a moment, processing the information. He had a daughter. His daughter had a *bedtime*. "Did you tuck her in?"

"Yes. I do every night."

That told him that an evening out was a rarity for her, which filled him with an oddly possessive satisfaction. He hadn't been a father to Lexi, but most likely no other man had been, either.

"Does she like to have a story read?" he asked.

"Every night."

"Let me guess—a fairy tale?"

Drew rolled her eyes. "It's her genre of choice," she said resignedly.

"Does she sleep with a teddy bear?"

In fact, Lexi slept with a stuffed frog, but Drew didn't know how to deal with Whit's wistful line of questioning, except to bring it to a halt.

"Look, Whit, this isn't making things any easier."

"I wish it could be easier, too," he said. "Too bad life isn't like one of Lexi's fairy tales." He was darned if he could figure out a way to conjure a happy ending out of this mess.

Drew's mouth quirked up at the corner. "I couldn't agree more. If I had a pet dragon, you'd be toast. The end," she said dryly.

He smiled at her words, but underneath them, he could sense that she felt threatened. He supposed it was natural. Still, he didn't want her to feel that way.

"Look, Drew," he said gently. "No one planned things to turn out like this. But it's not going to help if you and I don't work together. We share a common past. Let's draw on that to deal with the present."

Drew felt her spine stiffen. "What we shared in the past was a mistake, a mistake in judgment made by two reckless teenagers. Now that we're older and wiser, there's no need to compound it by making an even bigger one." She had been foolish enough to dream, and had paid the consequences; but she didn't want her starry-eyed daughter to have to pay a price that high.

Whit knew she didn't mean Lexi was a mistake. She meant their relationship had been, and somehow that hurt. "I couldn't agree more," he said evenly. Trying to fix that mistake had been why he'd torn his heart apart when he'd torn loose and left her. "There's no room to mess up, where Lexi is concerned."

She looked at him, considering. "You really want what's best for Lexi?"

"Of course. What do you think?"

She lifted her chin and faced him. "What do you think I'm thinking? Seven years ago you left Anders Point—and me—for the life you wanted. You've been in the spotlight ever since, moving from place to exotic place, woman to glamorous woman. You're the Prince of Hearts," she said, her voice rising with emotion. "Well, I'm Lexi's mother. And I'll do anything in this world—anything!—to protect her from being hurt."

Her eyes flashed green fire as she pointed a finger at his chest. "So now that you've come back, Your Highness, you'd better listen good. Because over my dead *body* will I let you use my daughter, who has enough to deal with right now without being in the center ring of an international media circus, as some toy you're going to lay claim to and play with for a while and then toss aside," she warned. "Because when you leave—and you will—that'll leave *us* to deal with the real-people, lifelong consequences."

While she spoke she could see the muscles in Whit's jaw flex and harden, but he said nothing. He just got to his feet and turned away from her.

Whit mentally swore a string of oaths in languages that spanned half the globe. Then he went over to the liquor cabinet and poured himself two fingers of something good and strong—no—three. He tossed it back and felt it sear his insides, but not as much as Drew's words had.

The strange thing was, even burned by it, he still grudgingly admired the fire in her. Her flaming temper, her spark of enthusiasm, her smoldering passion were all the things that had drawn him to her. He had been her first lover, but her honest hunger for him had driven him to a heat he had never experienced with another woman, ever. Other women tried too hard or were too circumspect, both too self-conscious and too conscious of his position. But not Drew; she was an elemental woman.

As the bourbon mellowed him, Whit forced himself to look at her outburst not as an attack on him, but as a valiant defense of her daughter. As elemental a force as a male hungering for his female was the instinct of a mother to protect her child.

He gazed out of the library window, out across the ocean. Looking at it from her viewpoint, Drew had reason to feel threatened by him. As she had pointed out, he *had* left her, and they both knew why. It was also true that he had gone on to earn his well-documented reputation as a man who went from woman to woman. As for that, only he knew why.

He turned back around and gave Drew a long look. He had to admit that time had done little to change the girl he had known in the first blush of womanhood, except to make a few improvements. The blond hair that she had worn long then was now cut in a short, sassy style that suited her personality. Her green eyes held even more mysterious shadows, and her lips had achieved a lush fullness. The same might be said for her body: she was still petite and trim, but the gentle curves that had enthralled his unskilled hands had swelled into even more tempting proportions.

Dismayed at the direction his thoughts were taking, Whit swore inwardly and took his seat again. After taking a deep breath, he spoke.

"It is true that I left you," he began quietly. Leaving her when things got serious was the one noble, princely thing he had done in his entire life.

And staying to figure out what was best for their daughter was going to be the second.

He went on. "But everything else you said was pure speculation. I'm not going to waste my time denying it, because I've always believed that a man should be judged by his actions, not his words." He looked at her, straight-on. "And you have the right to judge me, Drew, from this moment on, when it comes to Lexi."

"What are you saying, Whit? What exactly is it that you want?"

He ran his fingers through the long waves in his hair. "I honestly don't know," he said. "I just found out today that I'm her father."

Drew swallowed. "It sounds like you're thinking that you might want to be Lexi's father—in more than just the biological sense."

"Yeah, I guess I am." He might have felt differently if he hadn't seen his daughter today—Whit didn't know. All he knew was that seeing Lexi, coming to her rescue, and then that kiss—he felt somehow that Lexi needed him. Him, Whit Anders. He couldn't explain that to Drew; hell, he really didn't understand it himself. But he had to find out what Lexi needed from him.

Drew's reply was determined. "Don't even think about trying to get custody. Lexi belongs with me. I'll fight you to my last gasp to keep her."

"Drew, I don't want to take her away from you. You're her mother. That's something I could never be, even if I wanted to."

Neither spoke for a few moments. It was a heavy silence, made heavier when Drew quietly asked, "Do you really want to be a *father?*"

The weight of the past bore down on Whit. Seven years ago his answer to that question had been an honest and emphatic *no*. Learning that Drew dreamed of having a family had been a harsh wake-up call for him. She had wanted it all—and deserved it all—but there had been no way he'd felt up to taking on that magnitude of responsibility. He'd been having a hard enough time just trying to live up to his responsibilities as a prince without another major screwup.

But that was then, and this wasn't a hypothetical question anymore. He had a daughter, a real person with a name and a face and a dangerous knack no one else had ever had for reaching out and touching his heart.

No one else except the little girl's mother, that is.

Watching Whit, Drew swallowed. This was it in a nutshell. She'd had no choice but to throw the past up in his face, because their past was terribly important to Lexi's future. On their last night together, when neither of them had known that nature was bonding them together as parents, the issue of parenthood had torn them apart as lovers. The simple truth was that he hadn't wanted to be a husband and father, and he had admitted that then. And if he still didn't want to be a father, as she felt sure was the case, far better to come to terms with it now, before this went any further than the two of them.

"Do you, Whit?" Drew asked again. "Do you

want to be there with Lexi and for her, day after day, in good times and bad? Never to leave, even when the going gets so rough it's all you can think of doing? To be a part of her life and her future, forever?''

Whit met her gaze. ''Look, Drew. I don't know if a guy like me could ever fill the traditional father role. Gut instinct tells me no. Lord knows I've screwed up enough already. But gut instinct also tells me that there is some role I should play in Lexi's life.''

Drew had to admit to herself that Whit was taking a reasonable approach to this. If only she could be so reasonable. But this was Lexi they were talking about! No wonder her emotions had a stranglehold on her reason.

He asked quietly, ''Has she ever asked about me?''

She rubbed her fingertips on the smooth arm of the chair. ''Lexi hasn't asked as many questions about her father as you might expect,'' she said. ''They tended to be general, and I always answered them in a general way. I talked about families, and told her honestly that some kids lived with both parents and some didn't. She knows that I didn't grow up in a house with my father, either. And she isn't the only kid on the Point who lives with just one parent.''

''How did she take it?''

Drew shrugged. ''Kids tend to take things like that for granted. She never knew any different, so she was always content with the way things were.''

''You're pretty good at this mom stuff.''

She looked him in the eye. ''It's not easy, Whit.''

''Like when she asked if I was a stranger?''

She sighed. ''Sometimes you just cross your fingers and go on instinct.''

"Maybe that's what we should do. After all, we don't have to decide the future in one night."

"I know what my instincts are telling me," Drew said. But he had already ruled out disappearing. "What are yours telling you?"

Whit pondered that for a moment. "To get to know Lexi, and let her get to know me."

"As her father?"

He shook his head. "She doesn't have to know that now, and neither does anyone else."

Drew's eyes narrowed with suspicion. "Are you saying you're not going to tell anyone about this?"

"Not even my father or brother, if that's the way you want it."

Drew found she couldn't resist a parting shot. "No trumpets, no fanfare, no juicy interviews with the tabloids?"

Whit bit back a sharp reply. "Drew," he said evenly, "I'm tired of saying that I want what's best for Lexi. It's time to let me prove it."

She was behaving badly, and she knew it. His leaving had hurt her, but he had never broken any promises, because he'd never made any. More accurately, she had hurt herself. Her love for him had been a light of pure hope shining into the heart of a girl who hadn't had much love in her life. She'd hurt herself with the glowing expectations for a happy future together that she had deceived herself into believing could come true. And when she had shared her dreams with him, lying there in his arms under the stars on their last night together, he had had the guts to be honest with her. She had no right to be angry with him, but she had every right to be cautious, for

Lexi's sake—because Lexi's dreams cast him in the same unwanted role that hers had.

Still, as Lexi's father he no doubt had legal rights, rights that he might insist on if she didn't agree to his request. On the surface what he wanted was more reasonable than she might have expected. And what choice did she really have?

"All right," she said at last, rising from her chair. "We'll give it a try this way. Just letting you two get to know each other through the natural contact Lexi and I would have with an old friend of mine."

He felt relief pouring through him. "When?" he asked, getting to his feet.

He must have sounded too eager, because she pulled back visibly. Before she could answer, he offered, "How about if you make the first move?"

"All right."

The negotiations were over. The moment cried out for a handshake, but what they had once meant to each other made contact awkward. Whit waited. As the woman, it was Drew's place to make the first move. At last, slowly, she held out her hand.

He took it, but instead of letting go, covered it with his other one. Her hand seemed to shrink from his touch. He held on to it, wanting her attention, wanting to give her something that would strengthen the oh-so-fragile trust she had reluctantly given him tonight.

"Before you leave, Drew, there's one more thing I want to say. I'm glad for this chance to get to know Lexi, and maybe to find some kind of role in her life. But like you said, you're her mother, and from what I can tell, you're a darned good one. I want you to know that if there's ever a question as to what's best for Lexi, you have absolute say."

"Thank you for that," Drew said in a choked whisper. Without looking at him again, she pulled her hand back and left the castle.

Whit knew she wouldn't appreciate an offer to walk her home, but he wanted to make sure she got there safely, anyway. After a few minutes, when she was partway down the hill, he headed out to the gate in the big iron fence that surrounded the castle. From there, by the glow of her distant porch light, he saw her go in the front door of her house.

He took his time going back inside the castle, knowing that no matter how much he wanted to follow Drew into that house where his daughter lived, there was nothing he could do. Except wait.

Whit was outside tuning up his motorcycle the next afternoon, when he spotted Drew and Lexi walking up the castle drive. Or, more accurately, Drew was walking. Lexi was skipping, then stopping to examine something in the grass, then running, then bending down to retrieve the crown that had fallen off her head, then looking up at him and waving.

Grinning, he waved back. He had just finished wiping the grease off his hands with an old rag when they approached.

Lexi stopped skipping and gave him a solemn look. "Greetings, oh prince," she said, curtsying.

He wanted to laugh, not at her, but with delight. But he stifled the urge.

She broke into a wide, sunny smile. "I heard that in a story once," she said. "Do you like people to say that to you, instead of plain old 'hi'?"

He returned her grin. "Princess Lexi, you may greet whatever way you wish, as long as it's often."

He looked up at Drew, who was trying to mask a look of nervous apprehension. "Plain old hi," he said softly.

"Plain old hi to you," she returned, and he thought he saw her relax a bit before Lexi reclaimed his attention.

"What are you doing?" she asked.

"Working out some of the kinks in the engine."

"Why don't your servants do that?"

He laughed. "I don't have any servants, Lexi."

"Why not? You're a prince."

"But this isn't long ago. When I need help, I hire someone and pay wages. Then they are on my staff."

"Oh. Like Mr. Sloane?"

Sloane had returned that morning, and Whit had to admit that the young man was starting to grow on him—when he wasn't being irritating, that is. "My father gets the credit for hiring him," he said wryly.

"I met King Ivar at Julie's wedding. He let me wear his crown. Why aren't you wearing your crown?"

"Want to know a secret?" he asked her.

"Yes!" she declared, her green eyes shining. "I'm good at secrets."

"I don't have a crown."

"You don't?" Her disappointment was plain. "Why not?"

"Only the king does."

"Oh," she said. Then she perked up. "Well, I have one. Do you like it?"

He took a good look at it, walking all the way around her. "Yes," he said finally. "It looks light and comfortable, and I like the craftsmanship."

"What's that?"

"The way it was made."

"Oh. Well, it was made with foil. That's why it's so shiny."

"I can see that," Whit said. "Did you make it yourself?"

"Yes. I always make my own crowns."

"Well, if that's the kind of work you do, I may ask you to make one for me."

She looked up at him doubtfully. "I don't think I have that much foil," she said.

He laughed.

"Anyway, do you know why we came?" she asked.

"I hope you don't need a reason to come and visit me in my castle, Princess Lexi."

"Well, our reason this time is cookies."

She wanted cookies? He wondered if there were any in the castle, and if so, where they would be. He hadn't paid any attention to what was on the pantry shelves, and Sloane was out getting the limo serviced.

Then Drew held out a box. "We always bake cookies when a new neighbor moves in," she explained.

Whit smiled at her, then at Lexi. "I'm honored, even though I'm not really new."

"You are to me," Lexi said. "So you get cookies. And plus I like you."

Whit felt his old heart rocketing around in his chest. "I like you, too," he said. "Would you do me the honor of joining me for cookies and milk?"

Lexi turned to Drew. "Can we, Mommy?" When her mother hesitated, she said, "I mean, may we? Please?"

"All right," Drew said. She followed the two of them into the castle, trying not to resent how much her daughter already liked Whit, or how she herself was already feeling left out.

"You *would* have to be a prince," she grumbled to Whit as he held the kitchen door open for them.

"It's not like it was my choice," he murmured back.

Lexi had heard them. "You were born a prince, weren't you?" she asked Whit.

"That's right," he said. "Just like I was born left-handed."

Lexi's eyes opened wide. "I'm left-handed, too!" she said.

Whit and Drew exchanged a quick look. Wondering what other genetic traits he had given his daughter, he seated Drew first, pulling out a chair for her. He put Lexi next to her, at the head of the table. Then he washed his hands and fumbled around the kitchen until he had found a glass and a plate for each of them, and the milk.

Surprisingly, he took a seat on Drew's other side. She had expected he'd want to follow up on the inroads he was making by sitting next to Lexi, instead of putting herself between them.

They munched cookies in silence until Lexi started asking Whit more questions. "Have you ever rescued a damsel in distress?"

"Lexi, Whit is not a fairy-tale prince," Drew said pointedly.

Whit swallowed some milk before answering Lexi's question. "As a matter of fact, I have."

"Really?" Lexi asked. "When? How?"

He looked at Lexi, but he could see Drew's reaction from the corner of his eye. She looked as if she wanted to stuff her cookie down his throat. "Oh, about fifteen years ago. She was up in a tree house, and her friend had taken away the ladder for a joke, so she couldn't get down. I put the ladder back up for her.''

Lexi looked disappointed. "That's it? That's all you did? Anyone could do that.''

"It might not seem like much, but that damsel was pretty grateful, at the time,'' Whit pointed out. He turned to Drew. "Weren't you?'' he asked.

Lexi's eyes widened. "He rescued *you,* Mommy?''

Drew smiled, evidently relieved that he hadn't played up the prince angle. "He did,'' she admitted. "I told you he and Julie and I played together when we were kids.''

"Was Julie the one who took away the ladder?''

"Yes, but she was getting me back for putting pine needles down the back of her shirt.''

"I'll bet you knew Prince Whit would rescue you, didn't you, Mommy?''

"I had to,'' Whit broke in.

"Because you're a prince,'' Lexi said knowingly.

"No. Because she was screaming that she was going to put pine needles down *my* shirt if I didn't!''

They all laughed. Another cookie later, Lexi had another question. "Prince Whit, did you ever slay any dragons?''

"There are no dragons, Lexi,'' he said gently.

"But you *would* have,'' she insisted.

"I don't think so. I've never knowingly hurt an animal.''

"It's true,'' Drew told her. "I remember he wouldn't even kill an ant when he was a boy. He had a dog he treated like a prince, too,'' she recalled, changing the subject. "Whatever happened to him?''

Whit smiled, pleased that she had mentioned his old friend. "He was with me until last year."

"Where is he?" Lexi asked.

To his surprise, he found that he wanted to shield her from this hard truth, so remote from her. But he answered her honestly. "He died."

Lexi's face clouded over. "Didn't you take him to the vet?"

"Yes, but the vet couldn't make him better, princess."

"Why didn't you get a royal magician to cast a spell, so your dog would live?"

"No one can do magic like that, Lexi," he said. "But the vet helped make him feel better, before he died."

There was compassion in Drew's gaze as she spoke to Whit. "I'm sorry," she said. "I know how special he was to you."

"Thanks," he said, and meant it. She had been one of the few people who had understood that bond. He looked at Lexi and tried to coax a smile out of her. "Do you have any pets?"

"No," she said, but she did brighten a little. "But I love dogs. I played with Rufus when he lived here with Prince Erik. And Mommy says maybe I can have a pet when I'm a little older."

"I hope you can. Every kid should have a special playmate."

"Can I have you?" she asked, leaning forward eagerly. "You're a playboy."

He was shocked out of a reply.

"Well, you must be!" Lexi insisted. "I heard my mommy say it to Annah once."

Drew, he noticed out of the corner of his eye, had

the grace to blush. And Lexi, luckily, had heard the word but obviously missed its meaning.

"But most important is that you're a prince." She looked up at him through her lashes. "You see, I could really use a prince," she said wistfully.

Whit looked at Drew, who was shaking her head. Then he turned back to Lexi, who sat there looking serious and hopeful. He couldn't just ignore her. "So you need a prince," he said cautiously. "What for?"

"Oh, for lots of things." She folded down her fingers as she spoke. "Rescuing me, defending me, doing my bitting...just like in the stories."

Drew rolled her eyes.

Whit smiled at Lexi. "I've never been much good at doing anyone's bidding but my own," he admitted.

"Well, that's not the most important thing. Fighting for me is, and being noble and princely and all that stuff. My prince would be very special."

Whit felt the old discomfort with his prince role arise. He wasn't most people's idea of a prince, much less the fairy-tale prince on a white charger who saves the kingdom, which was the kind that Lexi expected him to be. "Maybe I wouldn't be good at those things," he said. "Maybe I'm not the prince you're looking for."

"Maybe not. But if you are, I'll know it," she said confidently. "Do you want to try?"

Drew got up from the table. She did *not* want him to be Lexi's prince, but Lexi had other ideas. And Whit seemed to be waffling. "It's time we got going and let Whit get back to his work," she told Lexi.

Lexi stood up, too, and went over to Whit's chair.

"Remember yesterday when you said you were at my service?"

That reminder decided it. Rescuing, defending, fighting for her—he knew he would do those things in a minute, remembering how he'd felt after the incident at school. Of course, Drew wouldn't like the idea. But he would do it anyway, because this was what Lexi needed. A princely role wasn't quite what he'd had in mind, but it was a role in her life. It was doing what needed doing.

"I'll do my best, princess," he told Lexi.

Drew glared at him while the three of them left the kitchen together, not that he let on that he noticed. As they walked outside, she asked him, "What brings you to the Point, anyway?"

"My father sent me here," he said. Though heaven only knew what for, and heaven wasn't telling any more than his father was. He felt as if he was being tested yet again, and this time he had no clue what he was expected to do.

"When will you be leaving?"

Lexi looked up sharply at her. "Is the prince going to leave?"

"I'm sure he will, honey," Drew said gently. Sometimes the truth hurt, but the truth was what her daughter needed.

Lexi turned to Whit. "*Are* you going to leave?"

Right then, looking into her solemn little face, Whit could have sworn that he'd never leave her. But what were the chances of that, realistically? He didn't know. All he really knew was that he wouldn't leave until his role as her father was resolved. It cost him something, but he gave her the most honest answer he could. "I always have, princess."

Though his words filled her with painful memories of their last night together, Drew gave silent thanks.

Whit had told the truth—more, he had made no apologies or excuses for the way he was. The same as when he had left her.

Lexi, though, saw his answer differently. "Well, just because you always *have* doesn't mean you always *will*," she said cheerfully.

Neither Whit nor Drew made a reply to that one.

"What should I call you?" Lexi asked Whit when they reached the gate at the end of the drive. "Prince Whit like you said in the gym, or Whit like my mommy calls you, or the Prince of Hearts like they call you on the news, or Mr.—"

"Anders," Drew supplied.

"Or Mr. Anders," Lexi said, "or Your Highness, or—"

Or Daddy, Whit thought, as his heart skipped a beat. His gaze collided with Drew's, and he knew the same thought had just crossed her mind, although with a far different effect. Shadows had crowded all of the sparkle out of her green eyes.

"What would you like to call me?" he asked Lexi.

"Prince Whit," she said, which settled that.

Whit stood at the gate, watching them start down the castle road. After one step Lexi turned around. "Prince Whit! I forgot to ask you something!"

"Are you sure?" he said with a wry smile. "I thought you covered just about everything."

"Oh, no. I forgot to ask if you ever woke up any sleeping princesses."

Drawn by a force greater than their mutual wish to act indifferent to each other, Drew and Whit's eyes met, revealing plainly that both were thinking about those midsummer nights when he had come to her bedroom window. Caught in a sensual spell cast long ago, neither moved, neither looked away.

Of course he had woken a sleeping princess. He had given her the kind of kiss that came straight from the soul. But what he had awakened was a feeling deep inside himself, a feeling that he had torn himself apart trying to deny. It was a feeling that, right now, he was afraid might be slowly reawakening, if the ache that was burning inside him was any indication. He would need to employ his best efforts to keep it dormant in order to stave off even greater pain.

"Did you, Prince Whit?" Lexi asked.

"I thought I did, a long time ago," he finally said, still holding Drew's eyes with his. "But I'm afraid I must have been dreaming."

"Do you think he was, Mommy?" Lexi asked.

With difficulty Drew pulled her eyes away from his. Swallowing, she turned to her daughter. "Probably," she said, forcing herself to keep her voice light. "I used to have a dream like that, too. But in real life, I've found that a smart princess is better off not relying on the whims of a prince."

Chapter Four

Whit was riding his motorcycle past Drew's house the next morning, when something white fluttering at one of the upstairs windows caught his eye. He slowed down to get a better look.

It was Lexi, waving a piece of cloth. Grinning to himself, he cut the motor and parked, then walked across the lawn and stood under her window.

"Good morning, Princess Lexi," he said.

Her head bobbed down and then reappeared, a sure sign that she had just curtsied. "Good morning, Your Highness."

"What are you doing?"

"I'm a damsel in distress," she explained. "I didn't have a kerchief to wave out of the tower window, so I used my pillowcase. I knew you'd come."

"How did you know that?"

"You're at my service, remember? So when I need you, you come to me."

She had much more faith in him than he had in

himself. "Well, it was lucky I happened to be driving by, right when you needed me," he said cautiously.

"And it was lucky I heard your motorcycle so I knew when to wave my pillowcase," she returned matter-of-factly.

Whit ducked his head down so she wouldn't see him smiling. He'd be darned if his kid wasn't cute. Smart, too. "Why exactly are you in distress, fair damsel?" he asked, looking back up at her.

"I'll tell you when I come downstairs," she said.

"All right," he said. "But I want you to promise me that you will never, ever lean out of that window."

"I wasn't leaning! I just stuck the pillowcase out."

"I know. Promise, anyway."

Lexi crossed her heart with the fist that still clutched the pillowcase. "Promise," she said solemnly, then disappeared. A moment later she opened up the front door and balanced on the top step, her bare toes peeking out from underneath a long, frilly pink nightgown. She clasped her ever-present crown to her blond head with one hand and waved him over with the other one.

"What is it that you need, princess?" he asked.

She grabbed his hand and pulled him into the house. "I need someone to watch cartoons with," she said, closing the door behind them.

"I see," he said gravely. "Just the job for a prince."

She nodded, and took his hand again. "In here," she said, leading him into the living room.

"Where's your mother?" Whit asked, looking around. It was the house Drew had grown up in, left to her by her grandmother, and it was as tiny as he remembered it. Living room, kitchen, bathroom and a bedroom downstairs, and, if memory served him, two more small bedrooms under the sloping roof upstairs. Drew was nowhere to be seen, but evidence of her was everywhere. Gone were her grandmother's fussy furniture, printed pastel wallpaper and voluminous lace curtains. These rooms were comfortable and functional, with furnishings of sturdy blond wood accented by a pleasing palette of bold primary colors. The backdrop of clean white walls and an overall lack of clutter opened up the limited space without sacrificing coziness. He felt at home immediately.

Lexi plunked down on the sofa with the remote in her hand. "Saturday is the only day Mommy gets to sleep late, so we have a deal," she said, pressing the button to turn on the television. "I don't wake her up until the clock says one-zero-zero-zero, and then she makes what I want for breakfast."

Sounded reasonable to Whit. "Are you sure she won't mind if I'm here?"

"Why would she?" Lexi asked curiously.

Not wanting to get into that, Whit sidestepped it. "Darned if I know," he said, settling down on the sofa. Lexi immediately scooted over next to him. Instinctively he lifted his arm up, and she snuggled against his side. Whit dropped his arm back down and forgot all about what Drew might think. Life as he knew it was receding dizzily away, like something you looked at through the wrong end of a telescope, but at that moment he couldn't have cared less. Sitting on a sofa in a tiny cottage in Maine next to a six-year-old child, His Royal Highness Prince Whit was sitting on top of the world.

Something told him that he was heading for a fall,

but that didn't matter, either. All the king's horses and all the king's men couldn't have dragged him away.

Drew woke up with the strangest impression that she had been kidnapped and taken to a deli. Levering one sleepy eye open, she saw the familiar surroundings of her bedroom. Everything looked normal. Stretching lazily, she inhaled deeply, then sat straight up in bed. Wrinkling her nose, she sniffed. She wasn't imagining it. Her house smelled...spicy.

She looked at the clock. It was late—almost eleven. She listened. The sound of Lexi's giggling coming from the living room was reassuring; except for the fact that it was punctuated by bursts of deep laughter that were very male and not very cartoony. What program was that daughter of hers watching? Why hadn't Lexi woken her up at ten, as usual? And what was that smell?

With her curiosity more awake than her body, Drew shlepped into the living room, running her fingers through her rumpled thatch of morning hair.

When she looked down, her hands fell to her sides and her mouth dropped open. Lexi was sitting on the floor with her legs under the coffee table, a plate in front of her. Next to her, stretched out on his side and looking perfectly at home, was Whit. They were watching an old black-and-white TV show, and laughing.

While busy gaping at them, Drew took a step forward—before she noticed that several flat cardboard boxes stood open on the floor. Her bare foot landed splat in the middle of one. She squeezed her eyes shut, hoping this was just a bad dream, but when she opened them, everything was the same—except that Lexi and Whit had turned away from the television to stare at her, and cheese and sauce were squishing out from between her toes while she stood on a pizza.

Lexi's eyes went wide. "Ooh, Mommy, that's just what the funny men on the TV would do... Moe, Larry and—" She turned to Whit. "Who was the other one?"

Before he could answer, Drew managed to speak. "What...is...this?" she ground out between clenched teeth.

"Breakfast," Lexi said brightly. "Do you want some, Mommy? I mean, for your mouth?"

"Breakfast?" Drew said, glaring at Whit. "This is your idea of *breakfast?*"

"Oh, no," Lexi said, eager to share the credit. "It was both our ideas, Mommy. I invited Prince Whit to watch TV, and at ten o'clock he said to let you sleep more, because you've had a tough week." She paused, her brow wrinkling in puzzlement. "I don't know why he said that, because it's been the *best* week. Anyway, we were both hungry, and of course, princes and princesses can't cook, so he asked me what my favorite food was and the pizza was my idea."

She smiled up at Drew, pleased at her inventiveness. When Drew didn't say anything she quickly added, "It has most of the food groups. I think. Mrs. Vittorini taught us about some of them yesterday. We're going to learn the rest on Monday. And besides, we had orange juice, too. Prince Whit poured and he didn't spill any."

"Congratulations," she said dryly, turning to Whit.

"Did they teach you that important life skill in prince school?"

He didn't answer. In fact, he seemed to be totally preoccupied with staring at her, but he wasn't quite making eye contact. Drew looked down and realized what she was wearing. With a gasp, she grabbed the afghan from the back of the sofa and wrapped it around her. "Why, you—" she began threateningly, before realizing that she sounded just like the three funny men on the television.

"Here," Whit said, handing her a stack of napkins from the coffee table. She stared at them. "For your foot," he explained. He looked so thoroughly innocent that she wondered if she had imagined the way he had looked at her a minute ago. She took the napkins numbly and leaned against the sofa, swiping at her foot. "Where did you get this, anyway? There's only one pizza place in town, and it doesn't open until noon."

He shrugged. "It wasn't a problem," he said, getting to his feet. "Listen, Drew—"

She cut him off as another thought occurred to her. "Oh, no. You didn't pick it up, did you? Of course you didn't. Princes and princesses don't pick up," she said, answering her own question. She gave him a horrified look. "You had it *delivered,* didn't you?" Pizza delivery in Anders Point was gossip on wheels. They delivered your order along with any juicy tidbits gathered along the way.

"Yes, but—"

This time Lexi interrupted him. "Mr. Sloane went and got it and brought it to us." She pulled the curtain aside and pointed out the front window. "See?"

Suddenly pizza delivery seemed entirely harmless.

There, standing in front of her house for the angels of heaven and all of Anders Point to see was Whit's limo—and in case anyone missed that, his stinking, noisy motorcycle was parked right behind it.

If this wasn't a nightmare, it was the next worst thing. Drew stared in disbelief. "Gary Sloane is—I mean, I heard that King Ivar had hired him to be the castle caretaker, but—your limo driver? You mean, that was him driving yesterday, when we…" She smacked her palm against her forehead and groaned. "Gary Sloane, of all people."

The doorbell rang, and Lexi flew to answer it. Gary Sloane, looking utterly professional and standing without slouching against something for perhaps the first time in his life, nodded briskly to her and then addressed Whit. "I saw the young lady at the window. Did you require my services, Your Highness?"

"No," Whit said.

The driver looked at Drew then, from tousled head to squishy toes. "Hello, Sheriff Davis. You're looking lovely this morning, as usual."

"Save it, Gary," she said.

"Is that a new kind of foot bath?" he asked. "Let me know if you like it, and I'll recommend it to—"

"No one," Drew said menacingly. "If you know what's good for you."

He gulped. "Yes, Sheriff Davis." He turned to Whit. "Will there be anything else, Your Highness?"

"No, Sloane. You may leave now."

Drew stared forlornly at the front door that he closed behind himself. "If I go back to bed, will all of this disappear?" she asked no one in particular.

It was a good thing she looked so lost and vulnerable, because that was what made Whit finally recover from the strong and very male reaction he'd had to seeing her appear, fresh from her bed. Rising to his feet, he took action. "Princess Lexi, how about if you go upstairs and dress while I help your mommy get cleaned up?"

While Lexi scurried off, Drew hopped on one foot to the kitchen. Whit followed, pulling out a chair for her. He found a towel and wet it at the sink, then kneeled on the floor in front of her and wiped off her foot, careful not to risk a glance up at her, even with the afghan wrapped around her.

He had memorized how she looked, anyway, every enchanting detail. She was wearing a men's ribbed white tank undershirt and plaid flannel boxer shorts, but the overall effect was incredibly feminine and sexier than the hottest negligee he'd ever seen—and he'd seen a few. The top exposed her smooth shoulders and scooped down just low enough in front to reveal the creamy swells of the tops of her breasts. What it didn't expose, the ribbing clung to, which was just as enticing. She'd looked warm and inviting and irresistibly appealing, and he'd had to fight back a primal urge to throw her over his shoulder and carry her back into her bedroom to touch, smell and taste every inch of her.

It was bad enough now, kneeling in front of her on the cold vinyl floor, cradling her foot in his hands while he gently wiped it clean. He moved one hand up to palm her shapely calf—ostensibly to gain better access to her foot, but even he wasn't buying that—and it was as warm and smooth as he had imagined, which made him wonder why he was torturing himself like this.

The feel of Whit's hand on her leg brought Drew

around at last. She was fully awake, fully aware of what was going on—and fully confused by the parade of emotions she'd been hosting ever since Whit had shown up at school. Here she was mad at him, and instead of letting him have it, she was letting him soothe her. His touch was doing such unbelievable things to her that she didn't even care that he was using a dishtowel on her *feet*. If that didn't look like a single woman starved for male attention, she didn't know what did! Well, she wasn't quite desperate or pitiful enough to have all of her common sense swept away.

She put her foot firmly on the floor. "Thank you," she said, in her most matter-of-fact voice. She was more than willing to ignore this whole attraction thing.

He looked up at her then, his heat-filled gaze making it difficult to ignore. "It was nothing," he said softly.

But they both knew that it was something.

Whit got to his feet. "You seem upset this morning," he said.

Drew stared at him. He really didn't get it. He was charmingly willing to clean up a mess, but not to realize that he was the cause of it. It was so—so irritatingly *male*. "Upset?" she said, her voice rising. "Why would I be upset? While I'm asleep my daughter invites a strange man into the house—"

"I thought we had established the fact that I am not a stranger."

"—to watch mindless television, and—"

"I was explaining all the finer points of the dialogue," he pointed out. "A lot of people miss those subtleties. Lexi caught on fast. She's got smarts, Drew.''

''Don't change the subject, although it brings up the relevant point of where she *didn't* get those smarts. A pizza for breakfast? What's up with that?''

''What's wrong with it?'' he challenged calmly. Drew had agreed to let him get to know Lexi, and that was what he was doing. If she didn't like something, he had a right to know why.

''I'll tell you what's wrong with it! It's not the way I raise my daughter. The television shows she watches are on PBS, and none of them involve hair pulling or eye poking. Breakfast is cereal or eggs or the occasional doughnut, but it does not involve garlic, oregano or tomato sauce! She wakes me up at ten on Saturdays because we have a schedule, an agreement. Her life has stability, something children find security in. Now here you come along and—''

''It was just a special treat, Drew. A little fun. Not a big deal.''

''Not to you, maybe, Mr. Prince Charming. But think about all the *fun* I'm going to have explaining why your motorcycle and limo were parked in front of my house on a Saturday morning!'' she said, getting out of the chair and standing face-to-face with him. ''This is a small town, remember? And your reputation—''

''Is irrelevant. We both know nothing went on between you and me this morning,'' he said irritably. His overblown reputation as a playboy was one of the major sore spots of his life. It was just a natural by-product of being a prince and not getting serious about a woman. He'd had a few lovers, but only one love. Ever. He had enough to deal with, just being around her again, without worrying about popular opinion in the town. "Let them think what they want."

"Your position may allow you that luxury, Whit, but mine doesn't! I'm a single mother who had a child out of wedlock. Ever since you left, I've kept my image scrupulously clean, and do you know why?"

"I can't imagine it's because you give a damn what petty gossipers say."

"You're right. But I *do* give a damn about anything that might have a negative impact on my daughter."

Whit fell silent, letting that sink in. She was right. "None of this is going to have a negative impact on either of you," he said, trying to reassure her. "I'll see to it. Anyway, I think most of the neighbors saw Lexi flag me down and let me in."

"The neighbors are the least of my worries. What about your driver?"

"Sloane? What about him?"

"Did you know that Gary has five, count 'em, *five* sisters?"

"He won't tell one of them, I promise."

Just then Lexi appeared in the doorway, all dressed and brushed, with a circlet of twisted pipe cleaners in her hand. "I'm having trouble with this crown," she said. "Would one of you please help me?"

Drew looked at Whit and raised one eyebrow. He backed off. "Looks like mom territory to me," he said. "And princess, it's time for me to go."

"Okay, Prince Whit. Thanks for getting me out of distress," Lexi said seriously.

"My pleasure. Let me know when you need me again."

She looked from Whit to Drew and then back to

Whit again. "Well, since you asked, I *do* have a problem," she said.

He hunkered down next to her. "Let's hear it."

"It's this," she said, digging out a paper from a pile on the countertop. "I want to play shrimp soccer."

Drew looked up from fixing the crown to stare at her daughter. That information sheet about the beginner soccer program for first-graders had come home from school at least a week ago, and Lexi had never said word one about it.

"Saturday afternoons, starting today," Whit said, skimming the information. "Sounds like a good idea to me, princess."

"But the problem is, each player has to have a grown-up," Lexi continued. "And the grown-up has to par… par… What's this word?"

"Participate," Whit told her.

"Yes and Mommy has a meeting to go to, the next four Saturday afternoons."

When Whit looked up at her, Drew nodded. "I'm coordinating a discussion group of women in law— police, attorneys, judges, prison officials," she confirmed. "Annah is going to watch Lexi for me. It's all arranged."

"But Annah can't do soccer with me, because we have to stay at her store, because Saturday afternoon is her busiest time," Lexi continued. She shook her head sadly. "So I can't play soccer. I don't have a grown-up." Then she looked up at Whit through her eyelashes.

"Well, if that's the only problem, how about if I—" he began.

"Thank you, anyway," Drew said quickly. She

could spot a prince test when she saw one, and this time she was awake to do something about it. "But we couldn't possibly impose on you like that." She looked at Lexi. "Honey, Prince Whit is a busy man. He probably has lots of other things to—"

"Not one," Whit said firmly. This would be a great way to spend time with Lexi, legitimate time together. And besides, Lexi was looking at him with those big green eyes. There was no way he was going to let her be disappointed.

"You mean you'll be my grown-up?"

"I would be honored, princess," he said, then he straightened up. "That is, as long as it's all right with your mother."

"Is it, Mommy?" Lexi asked hopefully.

Drew looked from one to the other and knew she was beat. Whether or not she liked it, there was no good reason to say no to this. In any event, not wanting to go public with this friendship between Whit and Lexi was not an issue. Thanks to her neighbors, Sloane and his sisters and all of the kids and teachers who were at that assembly on Thursday, anyone in Anders Point that didn't know by now that Whit was Lexi's prince would know soon. He might as well take her to soccer, too. And she had to admit that there might be an upside to Lexi's getting involved in sports—maybe that would get her focus off this princess thing and their lives back to normal.

"It's all right with me," she said at last.

"Oh, thank you, Mommy," Lexi said, giving her a big hug. "And thank you, Prince Whit." She hugged him, too, around the knees.

"You can pick Lexi up at Annah's secondhand store," Drew said as they walked him out. "It's in back of her coffee shop." He opened the front door, and his motorcycle caught Drew's eye. "And of course, you realize that you'll need a more suitable mode of transportation to take Lexi to the soccer field."

"Of course," he said. He winked at Lexi. "See you soon, princess." Then he whispered to Drew, "Don't worry. Everything is under control."

She watched him go, wondering who had everything under control. Because it sure wasn't her.

When Drew's meeting was over, she swung by Annah's house, in case Whit hadn't taken Lexi to soccer after all.

Annah lived upstairs, but after her divorce she had converted the bottom of the house into two businesses. She ran the coffee shop out front during the morning hours. Drew found Annah in the back room, which housed her secondhand clothing store. It was momentarily empty of customers—and, apparently, of Lexi.

"Hi," Annah greeted her. "Didn't expect to see you here."

"The session finished early. I take it His Highness, the prince, picked up Lexi?"

"Right on schedule," Annah said. She was putting clothes from the dressing room back on their hangers and returning them to the racks. "Didn't you think he would?"

The place was a mess, which told Drew that Annah must have had a busy afternoon. She started straightening up the shelves. "I just didn't know if he'd find something more suitable for the ride than that old motorcycle of his."

"He did," Annah said, looking amused. "Lexi almost went off the dial when he pulled up."

Lexi was entirely too taken with Whit, and Drew didn't know what to do about it. "She's wrapping him around her little finger."

"I know," Annah said. "Isn't it wonderful?"

Drew glared at her. "What's so wonderful about it?"

"Lexi's having fun. That's what kids are supposed to do."

Drew wasn't surprised by her comment. Annah thought Lexi's princess complex was cute. She let her try on fancy dresses in the shop and play the part. And Julie, who was a reading teacher, thought it was highly imaginative, and encouraged it by weaving tales of princes and princesses with Lexi. Even Lexi's teacher had said not to worry.

But Drew was worried. Especially now that her little princess had a "prince"—because when he left, that part would be no fun at all.

"What do you think about Whit?" she asked her friend. Annah had only met Whit briefly at Erik and Julie's wedding.

"Nice butt," Annah said with a grin.

Drew raised one eyebrow.

"Seriously, you mean?" Annah looked at Drew from across a dress rack. "Well, he seems like a nice guy. I pick up on a lot of energy in him, but all positive. Lexi lit up like a Christmas tree when he walked in the room, of course, but I swear he did, too. Seeing him with her, he sure doesn't seem like the dissolute playboy type."

"That's his reputation, though," Drew said. He

hadn't denied it when she'd brought it up, and he'd had the chance to.

"Playboy princes sell newspapers. I wonder how much the publicity has hyped up his image."

Drew had secretly wondered that, too, but what Whit had done since he left her really didn't matter as much as the fact that he *had* left her. She couldn't trust her judgment when it came to him. Annah, though—Annah was five years older than she was, married and divorced, and wise to the ways of the world. She had incredible insight into people, and that wasn't even counting the spooky ability to recognize true love that had made her a legend in these parts. Annah's thinking that Whit was a nice guy meant something; but then again, Whit had never broken Annah's heart.

"I don't like the way Lexi is latching on to him," Drew said.

"Oh, come on, Drew. What's the harm? Julie's like a sister to you, and she's married to his brother. That makes Whit practically family! Not to mention the fact that you two have known each other since you were in diapers."

Drew couldn't deny that. She and Whit had been friends long before the summer they became lovers.

Annah went on. "Lexi needs a male influence and perspective in her life." She paused. "If you don't like her getting close to Whit, do you have an alternative?"

Drew knew what she was talking about. From time to time Annah had encouraged her to reconsider giving Lexi's father a place in her life. Of course, even Annah had no reason to suspect that Lexi's father didn't qualify as an *alternative* to Whit.

"Listen," Annah said, strolling around to Drew's side of the rack and slinging an arm around her shoulder. "As I've told you before, you'd better watch out, girlfriend. Your life is as 'no frills' as they come."

When Drew opened her mouth to protest, Annah silenced her by saying, "I know, I know. You've had it rough, and you've worked hard to keep it all together. But you've got to ease up sometimes. Let Lexi have a little fun with her prince. Even better, why don't *you* have some fun with Lexi's prince, too?"

Drew backed away and faced her. "You've got to be kidding."

"I'm so *not* kidding that I will offer my baby-sitting services whenever you want to date the prince, fair maiden."

"If you think he's so great, why don't you date him yourself?"

Annah grinned. "I might, if he asks. But just for the fun of it. No sparks there."

Sparks were Annah's first indication of true love. "I thought your insight didn't work for you?"

"Well, it's never told me that a man was right for me, but it tells me loud and clear when a man is wrong for me."

"I have something that tells me that, too," Drew said. "Something called common sense." Never mind that it had kicked in a little late. Seven years ago it had been silent when she was careening straight down heartbreak hill, but right now it was telling her to steer clear of Whit. And she was listening. "Any woman with a fingernail's worth of it knows that a guy they call the Prince of Hearts has to be a bad risk."

Annah gave her a deep, scrutinizing look. "The trouble with common sense," she said sagely, "is that it's a handy excuse to keep from taking *any* risk. And sometimes it can make you miss out on an uncommonly good one."

Chapter Five

Whit had met all of the crowned heads of Europe, shaken hands with the heads of state from most countries on the globe and hobnobbed with the elitest of the elite. He could joke with paparazzi, parlay with billionaires, charm women who recognized him on the street and single-handedly defuse the tension at an entire social gathering to which sworn enemies had been invited.

But he was out-and-out nervous, sweaty palms and all, about taking a six-year-old child to soccer practice.

No wonder. He was out of his league. It wasn't the soccer part of it—he had played the game right up through college. It was the six-year-old child part of it. This was a real dyed-in-the-wool, authentic parent-kid thing, and he didn't know how he'd measure up—in Lexi's eyes, or Drew's...or his own.

He knew how he measured up in the eyes of his

father. As a prince and as a son, he had always been a bitter disappointment to the king.

It had been a burden trying to live up to the standard set by his responsible older brother. Erik always seemed to have it all together. He got the straight A's while Whit brought home B's. His father would shake his head silently over Whit's report card, evidently unimpressed that his second son drew praise from his teachers for the way he led class discussion and excelled on research projects of his own choosing.

Things had only gotten worse after Whit's mother had died, leaving him the odd man out in their family of three. His father became even less approachable and Erik, who had already begun to take on some of the duties of running the constitutional monarchy, shouldered even more and increasingly became their father's right-hand man. Whit knew that as the elder son, Erik would assume the throne one day with the approval of the citizenry, and that was fine. What hurt him was that his father had never asked him to do anything important. He got all sorts of varied little jobs, one after the other, that seemed more to keep him out of trouble than to allow him to contribute. He did them passably. Feeling so strongly the lack of faith his father had in him, Whit had a hard time putting his heart into them.

When he turned sixteen, Whit took matters into his own hands. Just out of college, Erik was assuming a number of the king's more visible functions, and the king was preparing to reassign his old duties to a trusted staffer. Hurt that his father wasn't even considering him for the role, Whit had plucked up his courage and asked the king for the assignment.

After long, long consideration, the king had reluctantly agreed to give Whit the job. To Whit's repeated assurances that he could take on this responsibility, the king had simply said, "Let your actions speak for you, my son."

That, of course, was exactly what Whit wanted. The job he took on was revenue collection, a paper-pushing, number-crunching, thankless task under the best of circumstances, but to Whit it was a golden opportunity. He would prove to his father that he could do what Erik did; not only that, he was determined to do it *better*. The present system was cumbersome and antiquated. Confident in his ability to find creative solutions, Whit threw himself into the project of overhauling the whole thing with new technology. When he was finished the system would practically run itself, and he would have earned his father's approval at last.

It might have even worked, had he been able to finish it. But while he was immersed in improving the future he'd let the present slide, and by the time he realized the problem it was too late to stop it. The result of his not doing the job he'd asked for had been nothing short of a national disaster. Without sufficient revenue, government workers hadn't received their paychecks and some programs had to be suspended for lack of funding. Whit's calamity made international news.

In an emergency measure his father had bailed out the government with his own personal funds. Whit had hand-delivered the paychecks to the government workers, knocking on doors and coming face-to-face with the families that had been affected in a real-life way by his not living up to the responsibility he had taken on. He would never forget the solemn looks on the children, whose well-being had depended on him. The whole thing had left him shaking.

Naturally the king had stripped Whit of his duties. Worst of all, he had done it without a word to his son—letting his actions speak for him. In misery, Whit felt the only punishment worse than the king's silence was the way he turned a deaf ear to his son. Whit had screwed up and he knew it. He wanted to take full responsibility for his mistake, but the king cut off all avenues for making amends. He never had a chance to apologize, explain or to show his father his project, which was on the verge of completion.

He was *persona non grata* for the next few years. In the wake of his failure had come that summer with Drew. And because of that, here was sweet and innocent Lexi, who looked at him as if he was every fairy tale come true. No wonder his nerves were raw.

Getting to the soccer field and finding that the father running things was an acquaintance of his from his former summers at the Point helped. So did the easy acceptance and camaraderie he felt from the other grown-ups there. But mostly, it was Lexi who put him at ease. Nothing got to him like her needing him, unless it was her absolute trust that he would be there for her when she did.

She explained to the other kids that she hadn't brought a mother or father, but that she had brought her prince, and instantly her stock had risen. Which was a good thing, because her play on the field didn't help it any. This was meant to be a series of skill-building sessions; next year, these kids could be on an actual team. Lexi was fine doing the drills with Whit, her partner. But she didn't seem very interested in the game, while most of the other kids were *into* soccer.

The kids were on the field alone at the end of the session, divided into two teams to play a scrimmage, when Whit saw Drew's car pull up in the parking lot. When she got out and started walking toward him, he felt a familiar jolt.

"How's it going?" she asked, standing next to him. She looked sexy as hell in her sunglasses, and he had to clear his throat before he could answer.

"Not bad. How was your meeting?"

He sounded interested, which pleased her. "It went over very well, which is a big relief to me."

"Why is that?"

He had his hair pulled back neatly and tied at the nape of his neck, which somehow made his eyes look even bluer. "Because this whole thing is my baby," she said, pushing her sunglasses to the top of her head. "I'm asking people to give up these four after-noons to participate, plus a three-day retreat next month. If it was a bust..."

"But it wasn't. Good for you, Drew."

They stood silently for a while, watching the kids chasing the soccer ball around the field. Lexi followed dutifully after them until her crown fell off, and she had to stop and pick it up.

"Not the first time that's happened," Whit pointed out.

"I tried to get her to leave it at home," Drew said with a sigh. "But at least I talked her into wearing sneakers and a sweat suit."

"It's okay. It's like her security blanket."

"I never thought of it that way, but I guess you're

right." Their eyes met, and he saw a hint of approval in hers that set off fireworks inside him.

They looked at Lexi again. She was still fussing with getting her crown settled back on her head. By the time she was finished, the ball and the crowd of kids after it had gone down the other end of the field. "It's funny how she was so interested in signing up for this, but she doesn't seem to even like it now," Whit commented.

"I've got news for you, Your Highness," Drew said dryly. "She's never been interested in sports at all. She did this to be with you."

"She did?" Whit knew he must have sounded as pleased as he felt.

"I just hope she can handle what she's gotten herself into." Drew was still looking out at the field, where Lexi was bending down to examine something in the grass. When the ball flew out of the pack straight for her, her teammates began shouting for her to get it. By the time she noticed, it was too late: the other team had descended on it and taken it in to score a goal. When the scrimmage was over, two of the kids on Lexi's team said something to her. From the look on her face, it hadn't been good.

That's why he was there: to help her handle it, Whit decided. "Is everything all right?" he asked, when she came over to where he stood with Drew.

"They said that I should pay attention," Lexi said with a long face.

That wasn't as bad as it could have been; in fact, it was true. Which Lexi as much as admitted, when she added, "You see, Prince Whit, I was paying attention to something else. I was looking for the little people that hide under blades of grass on soccer fields. They have a spell on them, and only the smile of a princess can set them free."

"I'd like to see that smile," Whit said, winking at her. When she grinned at him, he stuck his hand out. "Give me five, princess. I think you did a great job your very first time playing soccer," he said positively. "Don't you, Drew?"

"I only saw the end," Drew told Lexi. "But I'll take Whit's word for the rest. Good for you, honey." She hugged her daughter, but looked at Whit with worried eyes.

Lexi was beaming at their words of approval. "I didn't know you were coming, Mommy."

"I didn't think I'd be able to," she said. "But I'm glad I could. Are you ready to go home?"

Lexi hesitated, looking out across the parking lot. "Is it okay if Prince Whit takes me home, like we planned?"

Drew shrugged. "Sure, if he doesn't mind."

"Yay!" Lexi ran off excitedly. And then Drew saw why she was so excited. Standing at the edge of the lot was Sloane, in full uniform, holding the door to the limousine open for her.

From the look on her face, Whit could tell that Drew hadn't noticed the car before, hidden as it was behind a standing army of minivans. "You brought the *limo?*" she asked him.

"Of course," he said proudly. "And, believe it or not, I would have, even if you hadn't said something about the motorcycle. This is much more appropriate."

"Appropriate?" Drew looked incredulous. "Look around you, Whit. Do you see any other kids getting into limos?"

"No, but—" He cut off as she spun away toward her own car. "What is it, Drew?" he said, catching up to her. "What's wrong?"

She turned around and faced him, keeping her voice low. "You said you wanted Lexi to get to know you—but how can she, when you're so busy dazzling her with all the trappings of royalty?"

He ran his fingers through his hair. "I didn't think of that, Drew, honest. It was just a way to get her here."

"It's a way to get her, period." Drew looked meaningfully at the limo, where Lexi waved to them through the back window. Then she got into her car. "Go ahead, Whit. Lexi's waiting for you," she said quietly, before she closed the door.

Caught between the clouds in her eyes and Lexi's sunny smile from the back of the limo, Whit was sure of only one thing. He *was* way out of his league.

On Thursday night, one week after Whit had shown up at the Point, Drew heard the blare of a horn out in front of her house. Lexi jumped up from the dinner table.

"That must be Prince Whit," she said, dashing for the front door.

Drew followed right behind her. Whit had called her earlier to tell her that he was getting a family car, suitable for taking Lexi places. While on the one hand, Drew felt good about having gotten through to him, on the other hand, she was afraid that this rather big commitment meant he'd want to see even more of Lexi.

Outside on the front lawn, Drew skidded to a halt. Her mouth dropped open. It was Whit, all right, standing in her driveway next to his new car. But it wasn't a woody station wagon or a minivan or even a sedan. It was a screaming red convertible sports car.

He walked over to where she stood. "Well, what do you think?" he said proudly.

"This is your idea of a family car?"

He nodded. "Isn't it a beauty?"

Drew stared at him. "But Whit...it's a *sports* car!"

"Yeah, but it has a back seat," he pointed out. Lexi was, in fact, bouncing up and down on said back seat.

"It doesn't have a *roof*."

"But it has doors," Whit said, still defending his choice. "And it can have a roof, whenever we want."

We. That got to Drew, for some odd reason, although he could have meant anything by it. Still, it seemed that he had done this for *her*. After all, he'd been happy with his motorcycle; Lexi, with the limo. While she hesitated, he took her hand and led her over to the car.

"C'mon, Drew," he said. "Let's go for a ride."

"But I haven't even rinsed the dinner dishes."

"So what?"

"So that macaroni and cheese will be stuck to the plates like dried glue when we get back, and—"

"So what?"

"And it's a school night, and I brought work home from the office and...and it's cold out," she protested. It sounded feeble, even to her, but this *was* Maine, where, the old-timers always said, there were three seasons—June, July and winter.

He squeezed her hand, which sent a shower of hot lava through her veins. "Is it?" he asked in a low voice, and the look he gave her made her melt. "I've been feeling kind of warm, myself, ever since you walked out of the house.''

It was just like old times, when he could talk her into anything; when his enthusiasm was contagious, his charm outrageous; when just being with him made her feel more alive. Logic was irrelevant, because feeling was all.

"What do you say, Drew?" he coaxed, opening the passenger door for her, his blue eyes shining with boyish eagerness.

For no particular reason she felt the corners of her mouth start to twitch. It was a prelude to surrender. "Okay. I'll go," she said, struggling to look serious. "On one condition."

"What's that?" he asked, a tinge of wariness in his voice.

Enjoying having him off balance, she strolled around to the other side of the car. "I get to drive," she told him airily, sliding behind the wheel.

Breaking into a grin, he tossed her the keys.

The second week at soccer went much the same as the first. Lexi participated willingly—eagerly, almost—during the one-on-one drills with Whit, but during the scrimmage with the other kids at the end, her attention gradually waned.

Whit was standing on the sidelines, watching her and trying to figure out what to do, when Drew came up to stand beside him.

"Get out early again?"

Drew nodded. She didn't mention that she had gone to Annah's first again, under the suspicion that he might have not shown up this time. "How is she doing?"

"About the same. She's smart and she's quick and could do a decent job out there—"

"If only she wanted to," Drew finished.

"That's it in a nutshell." He frowned. "The other kids aren't any better than she is, but they're into it. She's not, and they're starting to ride her for it. It's the hardest thing to watch."

"Don't I know it," Drew said with a sigh. "But this is part of growing up. We can't fight her battles for her. Sometimes I think the best thing for us to do, as her parents, is…"

Whit knew why her voice had trailed off. It had hit him square in the gut, when she had started talking about him as Lexi's parent, too. *Us*. It was like she had accepted him as a partner of sorts, even if subconsciously. He stood a little straighter. "Is…" he prompted.

Her composure returned. "Is to stand aside and be ready to support her when she needs it," she finished.

"Get ready," Whit warned her, looking out onto the field. "Here she comes."

But when Lexi got to the sidelines, looking discouraged and on the verge of tears, it was Whit's arms that she flung herself into. He enfolded her in a hug that looked, to Drew, like the epitome of a safe refuge. It was the first time Lexi had turned to someone other than her for comfort. As he murmured to Lexi and stroked her hair, his innate tenderness toward her daughter—their daughter—made a lump of emotion form in Drew's throat. She swallowed, and took the hardest step backward she had ever taken.

After he had comforted Lexi and even coaxed a smile out of her, Whit settled her into the back seat of his convertible. He walked over to Drew, who was standing off to the side.

"That was really something," he said softly.

"The way you comforted her?"

"The way you let me."

"You noticed."

Sure as hell he had. Most of his attention had been focused on Lexi, but he had seen Drew's hands clench and unclench, had noticed her biting her lip, had seen the look in her eyes. She could have taken Lexi from him, but she hadn't. "Why did you do it?"

She shrugged, trying to look casual, but he wasn't fooled. "We agreed that you would do soccer with her," she said.

Whit knew there was more to it than that, but kept silent. He felt he had been given two gifts—Lexi's turning to him for comfort and Drew's allowing him to give it. "I promised Lexi earlier that I'd take her out for ice cream on the way home from practice," he said. "Why don't you come with us?"

She shook her head. "Can't. I just found out that I have to be in court all next week. Annah's going to be tied up with the remodelers she has working on her upstairs, so I'm going to try to catch people before they leave, to see if I can find someone to take care of Lexi after school."

It might have been her imagination, but Whit looked faintly hurt. "Why not me? Don't you trust me with her?"

"Of course I do," she said quickly, and it was true. Today had cemented the fact that when he was around, he took good care of Lexi. But this was Whit, and her main concern was that she couldn't count on him to be around. "It's just that..." How could she put this, other than stating the truth? "Every after-noon for a whole week is a big commitment, Whit."

"I can do it. I'd love to," he said.

"You'd have to pick her up at school."

"Easy."

"Help her with her homework."

"Cinch."

"Do some worthwhile activities with her. No spending all afternoon in front of the boob tube."

"No problem."

"Give her a nutritious dinner," Drew added, rais-ing one eyebrow in silent challenge.

Whit hesitated for a fraction on that one. "I can do that, too," he said.

"I won't be home until early evenings. You'll have to have her all ready for bed."

"I can do it all, Drew. Really."

Drew thought about it as the last of the other cars in the parking lot pulled away. Whit sounded so will-ing, but she had to be sure, for Lexi's sake. "It won't interfere with your work?"

He scoffed at that, playfully. "I'm a prince, re-member? I make my own hours."

"What are you working on while you're here, any-way?"

"Actually, the king hasn't given me my next as-signment yet," he said.

She thought she heard frustration in his voice, and it reminded her of all the times when he was younger and had had to jump to his father's whim. Apparently things hadn't changed all that much. Whit was so out-going and personable that most people didn't see his serious side. But Drew had. She remembered how deeply he had regretted messing up his one big assignment.

"What do you say, Drew? Do I get the job?"

He was giving her that heart-stopping smile of his, but she knew him well enough to know that this time, he was using it to mask a lot of hope and maybe a little fear.

There was no use trying to resist that. "Okay," she said, smiling back. "You talked me into it. You're hired."

He let out a whoop, picked her up and spun her around. Then he carried her over and plunked her into the front seat of his convertible, to Lexi's utter delight.

"Buckle up, girls," he said as he got behind the wheel. "Next stop, the ice cream parlor."

"And where after that?" Lexi asked eagerly.

Whit exchanged a look with Drew, one of naked honesty. "After that, who knows?"

Drew glanced over her shoulder at Lexi, who was looking at her with shining eyes. She reached back and patted her on the knee, knowing full well that her motherly touch was more for her own reassurance than for Lexi's. There was no telling where they'd end up going, with Whit at the wheel. But one thing was for sure. Until it was over, it would be one exciting ride.

Chapter Six

"Okay, my homework's finished, Prince Whit," Lexi said, looking at him eagerly over the completed work sheet she held out to him. "Now what are we going to do?"

It was 3:20, twenty minutes after he had picked her up at school, five minutes since Drew had called her house to check in on them. That left him just four hours and forty minutes until Lexi's bedtime—less if Drew got back earlier. Four hours and forty minutes to spend with his daughter.

"Whatever you want, princess," Whit said, grinning at her. He had come to this assignment armed and dangerous. Armed with a stack of fairy tales and coloring books, a soccer ball and the makings of a nutritious dinner. Dangerously full of the exhilarating knowledge that not only did Lexi need him in some mysterious way, but Drew did, too. Her way wasn't mysterious—she needed him to baby-sit, plain and simple. But needing was needing, and being needed gave Whit a golden opportunity to prove some things to Drew, to Lexi and, yes, maybe even to himself.

Lexi was looking for proof that he could be her special prince; Drew, that he could be a reliable daddy. Being with Lexi every day after school would give him lots of chances to prove himself—or to fail to do so, he thought, wincing. Living up to other people's expectations of him had never been his forte.

The memory of the disappointment etched on his father's face after he'd messed up the revenue job rose up before him. Whit knew it wasn't because of the money the king had lost; it was the fact that his son had failed him. Whit never asked for a duty after that, and it was several years before the king gave him the assignment of representing the kingdom at events all over the world. It was just another meaningless task, Whit knew; after all, Erik had never done it. But on the other hand, it would be hard, even for him, to screw up international partying and empty schmoozing. The perfect role for a misfit prince. And it had seemed like a good way to try to forget about the whole situation with Drew, and how he'd screwed *that* up too. Whit was good with people and enjoyed the public contact. But he felt keenly the grim fact that, in his father's eyes, he wasn't making a meaningful contribution.

Then his father had unexpectedly ordered him and Erik to switch assignments this past summer. It was the chance he never thought he'd get, and this time Whit had done the job right. He had dotted every *i* and crossed every *t* and run the whole friggin' kingdom by himself, while his father recovered from surgery and his older brother fell in love. Whit didn't find much intrinsic reward in the kind of work that the two of them seemed to thrive on; the satisfaction he derived from it was in finally proving himself to his father.

But his best efforts didn't seem to be enough for the king, who had exiled Whit to Maine as soon as he had recovered and Erik had returned from his honeymoon. Whit had done the job, but he still felt like a screw-up. His father had thanked him, but apparently couldn't wait to have Erik take over those important domestic duties again. And again, Whit felt like an outsider. Would he always be a second-rate second son? And if he couldn't be what his father wanted him to be, how could he be what Drew and Lexi wanted him to be?

Lexi eyed the coloring books and the fresh supply of new crayons that Whit had put next to them on the kitchen table. "Let's color," she said decidedly.

Whit bowed. "Would Her Highness perhaps like a horsie ride to the rainbow room of color?"

"Yes!"

Obediently he dropped to his hands and knees. Lexi climbed on his back and rode him up and down the hall and round and round the kitchen table before he deposited her, breathless and giggling, onto one of the chairs. Then he got to his feet. "Whew. The royal horse needs water," he said, getting himself a glass. "What would the princess like for her snack?"

"Cider, please," she said, busying herself with checking out the fresh, sharp points on the crayons. "And cookies."

He decided to have some with her, and then she coaxed him into coloring with him—Lexi doing the left-hand pages, Whit doing the right. He had hated coloring as a kid—all those lines to stay in!—but now, he found it oddly comforting and wholly absorbing. A half hour flew by before he realized it.

"How about we go outside for a while?" he proposed. Drew had said to make sure Lexi got some fresh air, and Whit was going to make sure she did. Drew was spending the week in court, but Whit knew that he was the one who was on trial. And so far, he was doing great. They had done the homework, had done the snack, had done the worthwhile activity. Outside was next.

"No," Lexi said, continuing to color.

"I beg your pardon?" Whit said, as if he hadn't heard correctly.

Lexi looked up at him and gave him an angelic smile. "No," she repeated. "No, thank you, Prince Whit."

"Why not?" he asked, frowning. "I brought a soccer ball. I thought we could practice some drills."

"I don't want to," Lexi said politely. "You said I could do whatever I wanted, and I want to color." And she went back to doing just that.

Whit was stymied. He couldn't get angry at Lexi; what she said was true. And she had been perfectly courteous about stating her preference. He himself had no objection to some more coloring, but the unfamiliar burden of parental obligation weighed heavy on him. What he was familiar with, though, was diplomacy. He was an old hand at bargaining and at finding off-the-wall solutions to problems.

"All right, princess," he said. "You can keep coloring."

"Great!"

"Until the dragon comes," he added casually, sorting through the crayons. "Hmm. Got any yellows?"

"Dragon?" Lexi asked, sitting up straight in her chair. "What dragon? When? Where?"

But no matter how much Lexi teased him to tell, Whit said no more on the subject. Eventually she settled back down to coloring.

Whit noticed that she wasn't working on one of the pages anymore, but on the blank inside of the cover. "What are you doing?" he asked, looking at the colorful network of shapes and swirls she was drawing.

"I wrote my initials, and now I'm decorating them."

He found the *D* for Davis, but in the ever more intricate pattern, he couldn't make out an *L* for Lexi. And he didn't even know his daughter's middle name.

He decided to remedy that one, quick. "Where's your middle initial, Lexi?" he asked.

She pointed to the middle of the paper, and he made out an *A*. "What does it stand for?"

"Annah, spelled with an *H* at the end," she told him.

"Like your mommy's friend Annah?"

Lexi nodded. "I'm named for her, my middle name. She was there in the hospital when I was born, since Mommy didn't have a daddy to help her," she said matter-of-factly.

She went back to coloring, while Whit pushed back from the table to try to yank out the arrow of remorse that had pierced his gut. He felt like the worst kind of villain, the ruthless prince who seduced an innocent young maiden and went on to other conquests, leaving her to face the pain of childbirth and the stigma of single motherhood alone. It hadn't really been like that, he knew. If he had known...but that didn't matter. The fact was that he *hadn't* known—

and hadn't been there. He wondered if Drew thought of him that way. He wondered if she had any fond memories of what they had once shared, or if that slate had been wiped clean the day he'd left her.

A moment later he had his answer. He looked at Lexi's picture again. "Where's your first initial, princess? I don't see any *L*."

Lexi giggled. "Well, that's because Lexi is my nickname. My real first initial is *A,* of course," she said, pointing to it.

"*A?*"

"For Alexandra."

Alexandra, his mother's first name. Drew's own mother hadn't figured much into her life, but she had always liked his; had, in fact, been almost as devastated at her death, when she was ten, as Whit himself had been. Still, if Drew had named her daughter after his mother, it meant that she hadn't hated him, even when she probably had reason to. Longing filled him, placing a stranglehold on his heart. What would have happened if he had stayed? Would he have been up to the task of caring for them—loving them?

Lexi got out of her chair and came over to stand next to him. "Are you all right, Prince Whit?" she asked, concern wrinkling her forehead. "You're all quiet, and you're not smiling."

He gave her a wink. "Never better," he said. Then he made his voice into a playful growl. "But you'd better hold on to your crown, princess. The dragon is here, and he's ready to play."

And with that he threw her upside down over his shoulder and carried her outside, gasping and giggling and ready to romp in the fresh Maine air with her prince-dragon.

* * *

As she had feared, Drew didn't get home until late. Although she was eager to see Lexi after the long day, she opened the front door with some trepidation. The house was quiet. "Hello. I'm home," she called out.

"Hi, Mommy!" Lexi called back. "We're upstairs."

Drew went up to Lexi's room. "See, I'm all ready for bed," Lexi said proudly. "Prince Whit ran my bathwater, but I did everything else myself, even brushed my hair, but I couldn't quite reach the bottom of it."

Drew tried not to get her fingers tangled in Lexi's long, blond hair while she gave her a hug. It would be a real mess by morning, but she didn't dare suggest brushing it out tonight, after Lexi had done it "herself."

"You did a great job, honey," she said, sitting next to her on the bed. She glanced up at Whit then. He was sitting on the opposite side of the bed, watching her. They were within arm's reach, but even that close, she couldn't read the expression in his intense gaze. Unconsciously, she lifted her hand as if to place it on his jaw. Luckily she realized what she was doing soon enough to change its course and smooth Lexi's bedspread instead. She prayed Whit hadn't noticed, but the look in his eyes told her otherwise.

"How did everything go?" she asked him.

"Just fine." He looked relaxed, a content smile playing at the corners of his mouth.

Lexi broke in. "No, it wasn't fine, Mommy," she said. "It was terrific! Prince Whit brought new crayons, and we colored all afternoon—"

"After she finished her homework," Whit put in.

"And then the dragon came—"

"Dragon?" Drew asked.

"He played with Lexi outside, in the fresh air," Whit explained, with emphasis. "Right princess?" he said to Lexi, and did his dragon growl.

She giggled. "And then we had dinner and Prince Whit told me stories about what it was like to be a prince," she said, eyes aglow.

As Drew might have expected. "What did you have for dinner?" she asked Whit, trying to bring the subject back to the mundane.

"Well, I *tried* steak and potatoes," he said, shaking his head. "I've seen Gustave, my father's chef, cook them a hundred times, but the potatoes came out kind of hard and cold, and the steak was—"

"Burned," Lexi supplied crisply. "Just like a dragon did it. So we had frozen waffles instead, and they were just right."

"You sure have a knack for mixing up your meals," Drew said to him. "Pizza for breakfast, waffles for dinner…"

"With lots of nutritious fruit on top," Whit added. "And milk to drink. Most of the food groups."

"And now," Lexi said triumphantly, "he's reading me a new fairy tale, and there's a prince in it, and—"

Drew raised an eyebrow at Whit.

"The prince is the bad guy," he pointed out. "The good guy is an ordinary woman, who is acting far more nobly than he is and is no doubt going to teach him a lesson by the end of the book."

He was looking steadily at her, and she returned his gaze. There were enough undercurrents in the room to suck a dozen lifeguards under.

"More power to her," Drew said finally. "Read on, Your Highness. Lexi, I'll come up and say goodnight after you're finished reading. For now I'll be downstairs, cleaning up the mess in the kitchen." She stood up.

"What makes you so sure there's a mess in the kitchen?" Whit said, with feigned indignation.

"Are you telling me there *isn't?*" she asked, calling his bluff.

His heart-stopping smile was all she needed for answer. Giving him a smug look, she headed for the door.

"Mommy," Lexi said. "Do you have to go to court again tomorrow? Can Prince Whit come back?"

Drew hesitated. The afternoon had been unconventional, but on balance he hadn't done a bad job. "He can come back," she decided. "If His Highness will help me clean up after he finishes reading."

"Will you, Prince Whit? Please?"

"Your mommy drives a hard bargain," he said. "I'll bet she wants me to wash dishes." He grimaced, which made Lexi laugh.

"But wouldn't you do it, to be my prince?" That question told Drew that her daughter hadn't forgotten about the prince test.

Whit got on his knees next to the bed and cradled Lexi's hand in his. "I think I'd wash them twice, to be your prince," he told her.

"Don't worry," Lexi said, settling back against her pillow with a look of satisfaction. "You're doing just fine so far."

Whit was momentarily taken aback by this praise. He looked at Drew instinctively, but caution made her change her instinctive reply to his unspoken question. Instead of nodding, she shrugged her shoulders.

After they finished dinner the next night—and cleaned up, this time—Whit and Lexi sat on the living room floor. The day hadn't gone as well, Whit conceded. He'd gotten a phone call from an acquaintance in the diplomatic corps who was looking for advice on a sticky political situation, and Whit had been turning the problem over in his mind all afternoon. Then, too, Lexi was grumbly from the time he picked her up at school. She finally admitted that she'd lain awake for a long time after he'd left the night before. He'd tried to settle her down to rest, and she had fussed about not being "a baby who needed a nap" for half an hour before inevitably falling asleep on the sofa. He'd had to wake her up for dinner, and that was easier said then done. Now she had eaten and was ready for bed, but she was wide awake after her nap.

"What do you want to do now?" he asked her.

"Play a game with princes and princesses," she answered promptly.

Tonight he wasn't sure he had it in him to play make-believe with her. Still, he didn't want to disappoint her.

"I have a better idea," he said, reaching inside the pocket of his leather jacket. "Let's play a game with kings and queens."

When Drew opened the front door, a little earlier than the night before, she could hear Whit's and Lexi's voices in the living room.

"Pair of deuces," Whit said. "Can you beat that, princess?"

"Read 'em and weep, Your Highness," Lexi piped up. "Two pair, jacks high."

Drew stepped inside and looked into the living room. They were sitting on the floor, across the coffee table from each other. Lexi was raking a pile of lollipops from the table into the lap of her nightgown, while Whit shuffled a deck of cards, a cigar dangling from his mouth. Lexi's crown sat on the top of his head at a rakish tilt.

He looked up and winked at Drew. "Welcome home, sweetheart," he said, Bogart-style.

"Hi, Mommy," Lexi said, turning around. "Prince Whit taught me a new game, and I'm cleaning up!" She turned back to Whit, who was dealing the cards. "Hey! You forgot to let me cut the deck."

"She's a sharp one, Drew," he said proudly, his teeth clenched around the cigar, and slapped the deck down in front of Lexi.

Drew didn't know where to start. "No smoking in here," she said, pointing a finger at Whit.

"It's not lit," he said. "Don't worry. Lexi and I had a long talk about the dangers of smoking."

"He never lights them," Lexi said gravely. "*Ever.*"

Drew looked at Whit, disbelieving, but he returned her stare and silently crossed his heart. "Then why do you have a cigar in your mouth?" she asked.

"It's just for luck, Mommy," Lexi added. "But it isn't working. I'm going to win."

"Big words from a princess who lost her crown on the second hand," he told her playfully, making a show of adjusting its position on his head. "It's mine now."

"I'm going to win it back!" she warned.

"Let your cards do the talking, princess," he said, dealing a new hand. "But first, ante up."

They both put a lollipop in the center of the table, then looked at their cards, disregarding Drew.

But Drew was in no mood to be ignored. "This is what you call a worthwhile activity?"

Whit sat calmly, arranging the cards in his hand and then discarding one of them. "If you would be quiet and watch instead of acting all indignant," he said in a low voice, "you'd see that this game is teaching your daughter about shapes, patterns, sequencing, probability and who knows what other mathematical properties. She's also learning about turn taking, risk taking and fair play."

"I'll take two," Lexi said, so absorbed in her cards that she wasn't paying any attention to their conversation.

"Two for the princess, one for the dealer," Whit said, doling out the cards. "But she doesn't know she's learning all that," he added in an aside to Drew, "because she's having too much *fun.*"

Drew sat on the couch to watch, and after a few minutes she had to admit that he was right. But she didn't realize she hadn't gotten around to telling Whit that, until after he had gone.

Later that night, with the old restlessness prodding him again, Whit got out the motorcycle and went for a ride. The night was restless, too—if it had been any windier, he wouldn't have taken the bike out—and dark with the kind of blackness you could feel, not just see.

At the end of the castle road, Drew's house pulled his gaze like a magnet. But it looked odd. All the lights were out, even though it wasn't so late that Drew would be in bed. Then he looked in the driveway and saw that her car wasn't there.

With a strange sense of foreboding, he stopped and went to the door. He rang the bell, knocked, called out, but got no answer—except from one of her neighbors, who was out walking his dog.

"They're not home, Your Highness," he said. "Went out about an hour ago."

Something was definitely wrong. Drew wouldn't get Lexi out of bed unless there was some sort of emergency. "Do you know where they went?"

"Nope. Left in a hurry, though."

Whit thanked him and took off for town with a roar of his engine. He tried to keep his pace slow, but urgency rode him, hard. As he had suspected, Drew's car wasn't parked at her office, so he started to head out of town, to the hospital. But then he passed her friend Annah's house. There were lights on there, so he decided to stop in and see if she knew anything.

"There you are," Annah said, when she opened the front door, sounding as if she had been expecting him. She let him into the front room where her coffee shop was. "Don't worry, they're fine," she added. "Lexi is asleep upstairs."

"Where's Drew?" he asked curtly.

Annah moved around behind the counter, calm but efficient. "She got an emergency call. The wind took a tree down, and it fell across the main road. There was an accident, and the emergency crew wanted her to help route the detour until they get the whole mess cleaned up.''

Whit felt his heartbeat start to steady. "Where?" he asked.

"Three miles north."

"Thanks, Annah," Whit said, then paused. He glanced upward, toward where Lexi was sleeping. "For everything."

She nodded. Somehow he thought she knew what he meant. He turned around and made for the door.

"Just a minute," she said, stopping him. "You can't leave without this, after I got it all ready for you to take." She handed him a big thermos and one of those waxed paper bags that bakeries use.

As he took them from her, he felt the hair on the back of his neck start to rise. He had heard the stories about Annah's inexplicable ability to spot true love, but he had never believed in mysterious insights of any kind. "How did you know I would be going to her?"

Annah gave him a slow, wise smile. "You tell me," she said. "Better yet, tell Drew."

When he got to the accident scene, the ambulances were long gone, two tow trucks were pulling away with cars behind them, and the road crew was just starting to clear the tree away. It was big enough to keep them busy for quite a while. He found Drew a mile further north, at the point of detour. She was all alone, a solitary figure in the windy, black night, looking vulnerable as she leaned against her car with her arms wrapped around her waist.

He wanted to wrap his arms around her, but handed

her the waxed paper bag instead. "Hello, Sheriff," he said.

"What are you here for?" she asked, eyes wide in the dim light from the flares she had placed on the road.

"For company." He put the top of the thermos on the hood of her car, poured coffee into it and handed it to her.

"You made coffee?"

He grinned at the surprise in her voice. "Don't worry. I got it from Annah. Not only will it be drinkable, it will be good. She also sent along something to munch on, in case you're hungry. C'mon, sweetheart, you must be half-frozen out here," he added huskily. "Drink up."

"What about you?"

"I'll have some when you're finished. Drink."

Drew was happy to obey this royal command. As she took in the warmth, she couldn't help realizing that this was the first contact they'd had that didn't have to do with Lexi. He had come here for her, and that made her feel warm, too, although she wasn't quite sure what he meant by it.

"Not a lot of traffic around here this time of night," he observed.

"No, but I have to stop each car individually. It's a complicated detour." She hesitated. Her sense of justice had been nagging at her all night, and here was her chance to appease it. "Whit, about what you said tonight—well, you were right. Not that I would ever have thought of teaching a six-year-old how to play poker," she said. "I don't even know how to play, myself."

Whit seemed pleased by her approval. "Anytime

you're ready to learn, you know who to come to," he said with a flash of a grin.

"Yes," she said dryly. "Lexi. She's the one who ended up winning her crown back from the Prince of Hearts, fair and square."

She handed him the empty cup, and he poured some for himself. "She's a bright one," he said. "Just like her mother. I remember when you had big plans. You were going to work your way through community college, then try to earn a scholarship. After you got your undergraduate degree you wanted to go to law school. You had a dream of being a judge some day."

Drew swallowed. She'd had a lot of dreams back then, not one of which had come true. "Dreams change. My *life* changed."

And he knew why. From the time she had known she was pregnant, every move Drew made was no doubt measured by how it would affect the baby. *Their* baby.

"We've got time. Tell me about what it was like, when you found out about the baby," he said. When she hesitated he said, "Start with the sale sign that was in front of your grandmother's house a few months after I left."

"You came back?"

He shook his head. "No. Erik saw it, and he told me, knowing that you and I had been friends. He heard that your grandmother had died and that you were looking to move."

"I wanted to."

"Because of the baby?"

She nodded. "I thought it would be…easier, if we got a fresh start, somewhere else."

That's when he knew that he hadn't pulled that arrow of remorse out of his gut after all. It still hurt like hell. "Why didn't you?" he asked.

"Because of the baby," she repeated. "Staying in the house my grandmother left to me was a big help financially. Until Lexi was born, I worked part-time while I finished my first year at community college."

"When?"

She knew what he meant. "May fourteenth," she said softly.

He silently committed Lexi's birthday to memory. "How did you manage, once Lexi arrived?"

"At first I used the savings my grandmother had left me, and I did my best to keep our expenses down."

"So you didn't work right away?"

She gave him that knowing smile that women had given men since the dawn of time. "I worked," she said simply.

She had him there, like women always had men. He liked how she hadn't made a big deal of it—he liked the implied intimacy of it, too—and smiled his apology. "I should have said, outside the home."

"It would have made things easier, moneywise, but I wanted to be with Lexi. And I wanted her to know that her mother, well, valued her."

Whit nodded. He knew exactly what she meant. Drew's mother had left her to go chasing after Drew's father. It was natural for her to want to give her own child something she hadn't had—and should have. He silently realized the blessing he had been given at birth—two loving parents. His mother had understood him better, and he'd missed her terribly after she'd died. As for his father—well, that had always been a rougher road, but deep down Whit felt his father cared about him in his own way.

Drew went on. "When Lexi was about one, Annah was just starting up her businesses. I had met her in the waiting room at my obstetrician's, and we had become good friends."

"I like Annah," Whit observed.

"Everyone does. I don't know what I would have done without her, because Julie only lived here in the summer, of course. Anyway, Annah let me work part-time for her, with very flexible hours. Which meant whenever Lexi was napping in one of the bedrooms over her shops," she said with a laugh. "In exchange, she stayed with Lexi on the nights I went back to school to finish up my associate's degree."

Whit felt himself swell with pride. If he had been consciously picking a mother for his child, he couldn't have done a better job. "In what?"

"Criminal justice."

So the old dream wasn't completely gone. She had just taken it in a different direction. "Then what?"

"When Lexi started kindergarten last fall, I knew I needed to get a real job."

"So you ran for sheriff and won."

"Unopposed," she pointed out. "And it's not as glamorous as it sounds." The position of sheriff of Anders Point had evolved over the course of decades and was, to her knowledge, unique to the town. "I do a lot of odd jobs, from picking up strays to parking cars at the Lobsterfest."

"Doesn't matter," he said loyally. "I think what you've done is incredible, Drew. I can't think of a better role model for Lexi."

Drew stopped her instinctive protest, and instead silently accepted his praise. It felt so, so good. And she had to admit that it meant all the more, coming from him.

"I'm glad you've had Annah to help you out," he added.

"She's a good friend. And Julie always helped me, too, when she visited the Point during the summer, and this past year, when she was caretaker here at the castle."

Whit had already shown his appreciation to Annah; he made a mental note to give his new sister-in-law a big hug the next time he saw her.

A truck came by then. It was the road crew, telling Drew the tree had been removed. After they pulled away, Whit helped Drew collect the detour signs. She let him, knowing it would take her twice as long by herself, or maybe longer. The cold hadn't affected Whit as much as it had her.

It never had.

Memories intruded on her, memories of other chilly nights, when he had shared a blanket and his body heat with her before making sweet, passionate love to her.

She felt his hand on her shoulder. "Drew?"

His voice was right in her ear. If she turned around, he'd be close, too close. So she got into her car instead.

"Thank you for helping," she said through the open window. "I—I'll see you tomorrow night, when I get home."

She stole a glance up at him. He said nothing, though his eyes watching her said everything. She wasn't ready to listen, so she turned the key in the ignition.

But as usual, running away from Whit never

seemed to work. When her car wouldn't start after several tries, she gave in to the obvious.

"I guess the battery's dead," she said. "I thought I noticed it was getting weaker." She looked up at him, biting her lip. "I guess I've got to call for help to get a jump, but I hate to get them out again, after they've just been here for the accident."

"Then don't. The car will be fine here until morning." Whit opened her door and offered her his hand.

She took it and got out. "But I've got to get to the courthouse tomorrow."

"You can use my car," he offered.

"I couldn't possibly—"

"Why not? I'll still have my bike and the limo. Sloane and I will come over and jump start your car in the morning—"

"But—" she protested.

"And then I'll put in a new battery."

That brought her up short. "You can do that?" she said, admiration in her voice.

He grinned. "Being a prince didn't stop me from getting this old motorcycle going, did it?"

"But it's not your problem," she argued. "It's—"

"Easy," he finished. "By the time school's out, I'll be able to pick Lexi up in your car, not the limo. Guaranteed."

There was no use arguing further. He was taking care of a situation that normally would have been a major hassle for her and seemed glad to do it. "Thank you," she said simply.

"No problem," he said, getting on his motorcycle and motioning for her to take the seat behind him. "Now let's go."

Her eyes met his, their expression unsure. He knew exactly what was bothering her. Riding double on a motorcycle was a forced intimacy, one that he himself would have avoided just two weeks earlier. But he had changed his mind, even if she hadn't.

"Come on, Drew," he said. She hesitated a fraction of a second more, then she got on behind him, sliding as far back on the seat as she safely could.

"Hold on," he warned, disappointed that she was going to hold on under the seat instead of around his waist. "And for God's sake, put on the helmet."

It was just like before, yet everything was different, Drew thought as she fastened the strap under her chin with fingers that shook. All the other times she had ridden with him, it had been along the coastal roads at dusk, with the wild ocean wind whipping through their loose hair. Now she wore a helmet while he drove at a decorous pace in deference to the wind and poor visibility. And now she sat keeping as much distance between them as she could without falling off—not plastered up against him with her cheek resting on his broad back, her arms wrapped around his waist, cradling his body between her thighs.

Then, the rides had always ended at some secluded spot where they had made love, wrapped so tightly in each other's arms that Drew couldn't tell where she ended and he began. This ride would end in front of her house, where they would go their separate ways.

Drew shivered. Her hands, numb with cold, were having a hard time keeping a grip. When he went around a corner, ever so carefully, he must have felt her shift.

He stopped the bike, dropping his feet to the ground. "Enough of this," he ordered over his shoulder. "I'm not going anywhere until you're holding me so tight that I know *you're* not going anywhere."

She did as he asked, and heaven help her, did it

feel *good*. He was even more solid than he had been then. Maturity had ripened his body, and he was every inch a man. She slipped her hands under his jacket for warmth, and found that she wanted to run them along his chest, wanted to explore the ridges of his muscles. She settled for wrapping her arms around him as tight as she could and sealing herself against him, absorbing his heat and strength.

She didn't notice at first when he pulled into her driveway; she was shut out to all sensation except the feel of him against her hungry-too-long body. Her house was surrounded by trees and bushes, so no one would see them there in the far corner of the driveway. She could hardly see him herself in the deep, dark of the night, as he got off the bike and then straddled the seat again, facing her this time.

He pulled her onto his lap, as he had done so many times, so long ago. Her arms went around him of their own accord, burrowing under his jacket. He brushed a kiss against her ear and then whispered, huskily, "We're home, sweetheart."

"Yes. I..." He was kissing her neck now, making it hard for her to remember her manners. "Thank you, Whit," she said at last.

He continued to ply her with soft, undemanding kisses. On her hair, her neck, her face. He hadn't touched her lips yet, but she knew he was heading that way. "What do you want to do about it?" he murmured.

Her insides were going all soft and mushy. "About what?"

"About this." His lips settled on hers then, warm and moist and mobile, and Drew became lost in an explosion of sensation. Here in this sensual glide of lip on lip was a comfortable familiarity that she had never gotten over missing, wrapped around a core of wild excitement that it seemed she hadn't fully experienced before.

An odd combination of relief and desire burst in him as her lips yielded to his, soft and pliant and welcoming his exploration. He felt he had been granted a key to unlock the past, to bring the best of it here to enrich the present. He ran his tongue over her lips slowly, then captured her bottom lip gently between his, remembering all of the secret caresses that she had loved. Her arms loosened the death grip they had around him, and he felt her palms gliding over his back, feeling him, measuring his strength; and at the feminine approval in her touch his masculinity seemed to increase.

It was no surprise to him that having her straddling his lap on the motorcycle had become too uncomfortable for him. He picked her up and got off the bike, then slid her down the front of him until she found her feet.

Still he held her close, and she huddled against him, using his body as shelter from the wind. He didn't seem to mind; in fact, he noticed that she was shivering before she did.

"Come on," he said, putting his arm around her shoulders and leading her to the door. "Let's get you inside."

Inside it was warmer—and darker and quieter. He stopped her hand as she reached for the light switch, and drew her back into his arms. He took off her jacket, which had never been warm enough, and led her into the living room. There he got the afghan from the back of the sofa and wrapped it around the back of her. He was keeping the front of her warm with his body.

"How does that feel, sweetheart?" he asked softly, resting his chin on the top of her head.

She nodded, because it was indescribable, the way he made her feel. For such a long time she had been a caregiver. Now she felt cared for. The only time she had ever felt this way was with Whit. Was it wrong to want to be pampered and made to feel so feminine, so special? Right or wrong, she wasn't sure she had the strength to resist. And she certainly didn't have the desire to. She lifted her face to his.

Whit looked down at her. "Right now I can think of a few things we could do," he said huskily. "And I think you could, too."

Oh, yes. She could think of *lots* of things they could do. He wasn't being pushy, he was letting her think about things. Although neither of them mentioned it, the knowledge that Lexi would be at Annah's all night hung heavy in the air around them.

"Things we've done before," he murmured seductively, "and things we've never dreamed of."

Drew felt a shard of reality graze her. It was a broken piece of the things she *had* dreamed of, long ago. Slowly, deliberately, she pulled away from his embrace, regretting the fact that her body had been making him promises tonight—promises that the rest of her could not keep.

"I'm sorry, Whit," she said. "But the truth is, I just don't want to start something between us."

He wasn't angry at her about-face. To her surprise he actually smiled at her, a gentle, rueful smile.

"Sweetheart, what's between us has been there a long, long time," he said. "It's not starting it that we have to worry about. It's whether either of us is ready to finish what we've started."

Chapter Seven

"**P**rince Whit! You just drove past my house," Lexi told him on the way home from school.

It was Friday, the last afternoon he would be taking care of her. "Today we're doing something different, princess. Call it a field trip."

"I know, I know!" Lexi said excitedly. "We're going to the castle!"

"Right, first try," he teased, winking at her. "I wonder how you guessed that, since we are driving up the castle road."

Lexi made a face at him. "Anyway, I love the castle. And I haven't played there since Julie married Prince Erik and moved away."

Parking the convertible out front, Whit was glad that she was happy about it—not surprised, but glad. She ran off to do some exploring on her own, which meant he could finish up some work he was in the middle of. Sure enough, when he went into the library, there was a fax waiting for him. There had been a number of new and disturbing developments in the international political situation that his friend had told him about earlier in the week. The two countries involved had not only made no headway in their dispute, but they had also broken off negotiations. Whit, being familiar with all the parties involved, had offered his services as an impartial negotiator. This fax was the second country's agreement that he take on that role.

Whit made his reply and did some more background research while Lexi ran in and out of the nearby rooms, her footsteps and happy chatter echoing off the stone walls. Having her there helped him work better, and he was beginning to realize why. Lexi had added a dimension to his life that brought it more into balance, that made the kind of work he was doing even more meaningful. That made his life more meaningful.

The fact was, not only did Lexi need him. He needed her, too.

Drew let the phone at her house ring ten times before she hung up and dialed the number again. Still no answer. She stood staring at the pay phone, wondering where they could be. But others were waiting to use the phone, so she stepped away and went to the end of the line.

Apprehension churned in her stomach. She had called at this time every day, and Whit had always had Lexi home from school by now. She pictured Lexi sitting alone out in front of the school, waiting in vain for her prince to come and get her. Had she talked to Lexi enough about what to do in an emergency like that, or would her daughter try to walk home all alone? Even if she made it, she wouldn't be able to get in. Drew's stomach churned harder, and she mentally berated Whit for being so—*irresponsible* didn't seem a criminal enough word. She had feared he would let Lexi down, but not like this! She would try calling one more time, and if there was no answer this time, she was hightailing it out of the courthouse, trial or no trial. There'd be hell to pay for that, but she was beyond caring about that right now. She had to find her daughter!

When it was her turn again, she listened to the empty sound of ring after unanswered ring before slamming down the receiver. Then, on impulse, she picked it up again and dialed the private line at the castle.

Whit answered.

"What are you doing there?" Drew asked. "Where's Lexi?"

"Having a snack," he answered. "Here, talk to her."

She heard some vague, crunching sounds and then Lexi's voice came on over the line. "Guess what! We're having soda and potato chips, Mommy!" Lexi said. "Isn't that a treat?"

Drew's heartbeat steadied at the sound of her daughter's voice, cheerful and unperturbed. After a moment she said, as calmly as she could, "Put Prince Whit back on, please." Her worst fears had been allayed, but the adrenaline rush that had pumped through her hadn't subsided completely.

Lexi, handing the phone back to Whit, said, "I think you're in trouble," loud enough for Drew to hear.

"Damn straight you're in trouble," she told him when he got on the line. "What is going on, Whit?"

He groaned. "Okay, Drew. I admit, it's not a healthy snack. But it was the best I could find, here at the castle. I swear, I think even *I* could do a better job of grocery shopping than Sloane does."

"Your labor problems are not my concern, Your Highness," Drew said through clenched teeth. "Why aren't you at my house?"

"I had some things to do here, and I thought the change of scene might be nice for Lexi. Is there some kind of problem with that?" he asked, sounding surprised.

"Just that I called home as usual, and got *no answer.*"

"I figured that would happen, and then you'd call here," he said, sounding pleased at his foresight. "And you did."

She plunked her forehead against the wall. "Whit, don't you get it? I was *worried!*" she said.

There was silence on the line for a moment or two, as if he needed to process that information. When he finally spoke, he didn't sound offended—although he might have had reason to, she realized, now that she was calming down. He hadn't let her and Lexi down after all; Drew had just been taken by surprise and had reacted on instinct.

"Everything is fine, Drew," he reassured her. "Really."

She took a deep, steadying breath. "I've got to get back inside."

"Are you all right now?"

"Yes," she said, touched by the concern she heard

in his question. "But don't ever, *ever* do that to me again."

As Drew walked over to the soccer field the next afternoon, the kids were in their usual end-of-the-session scrimmage. But Whit wasn't standing on the sidelines, as usual. She scanned the field and saw that he was running up and down the field along with the players, acting as referee. Lexi, to Drew's surprise, was running along with the other kids, too. When the ball came over to her side of the field, she found out why.

Whit was giving Lexi encouragement in a low voice, but he wasn't saying anything that would mean anything to anyone else, Drew included.

"It's almost midnight," she heard him say once, when Lexi had gotten distracted. "Hurry, princess!" And Lexi had run off after the ball. When she was tending goal, and the ball headed toward her, he said, "A rock has been catapulted at the castle!" and she caught the ball, making a save. And later, when the ball came to her out of a group and she had a break-away possibility, he had said, "Quick! The dragon is chasing you, princess!" as the other team bore down on her. She took off and dribbled down the field, and her shot on goal actually went into the net just as time ran out.

Lexi, who was mobbed by her teammates, waved to her mother, who waved back and smiled. Whit came up next to Drew, grinning from ear to ear.

"How did you do it?" she asked him.

"Well, we kept it secret, but Lexi and I practiced every day after school this week. Looks like it paid off."

"Practice wasn't all it was," Drew said. "I heard some of those things you were saying to her."

"Motivational phrases," he said, still grinning.

Drew swallowed. "I never would have thought of that," she said. "I would have told her to work harder, or pay attention; but you helped her to succeed by making it fun." Her voice dropped. "Thank you," she whispered, watching her daughter get high fives from her whole team.

"It was the least I could do," Whit said.

"What do you mean?"

"Lexi seems to have inherited my talent for marching to the beat of a different drummer. The least I can do is try to teach her whatever survival tips I've learned."

And that teaching, that passing of gathered wisdom from one generation to the next, was as important for him as it was for her, he found. That was part of what Whit had realized when he'd figured out that he needed Lexi as much as she needed him. He had never felt the way he did when he was with her, feeling her trust, her admiration of him. It was a new dimension of love for Whit, one that he hadn't known he was missing, because he hadn't known it existed. He had a feeling that if you put a name to it, it would be called paternal love, and it filled a large, aching need in him to shelter, protect and provide. He hadn't known that need was there before, or how good it would feel to fill it, but he knew how he would hate to lose that feeling, now that he had experienced it.

Lexi ran up then and flung one arm around each of them as Whit picked her up. Then Whit put his other arm around Drew, and she did the same, and they were linked together in a three-way hug, a family hug.

A rich warmth welled up inside of Whit, filling up all the cracks that had pulled apart in him when he had left Drew seven years before. This daughter of theirs would be special if only for the fact that she was theirs; but she was also special because she was Lexi. This woman would be special if only for the fact that she was the mother of his child; but she was also special because she was Drew.

Right then, holding them both within the circle of his arms, Prince Whit felt he had been given a privilege beyond measure. Which was why it was so important that he measure up.

That night at bedtime, Lexi looked out of her window after Drew turned her light out. "See all the stars, Mommy," she said. "More than I've ever seen."

It was a clear night, and dark there out on the coast, away from the lights of the town. Over the ocean, millions of stars winked and twinkled as if just for her little girl. "Do you want to take a walk down to the beach and get a better look at them?"

Lexi looked up at her, her mouth open in a small letter *o*. "Do you really mean it? Can we?"

"Of course we can." Drew held out her hand, and they walked downstairs and out to the backyard. Then Drew carried Lexi piggyback down the steep path to the tiny sandy beach below the rock ledge.

While Lexi searched the beach for the best view of the sky, Drew thought about that hug on the soccer field. That and lots of other things, too, like how happy Lexi had been spending the week with Whit. He didn't do things the way she would, but she had to admit that he had brought more than just a male perspective into her daughter's life. Lexi had learned a lot of new things that week, from how to eat with chopsticks to how to use a computer to how to play soccer. She had learned to play poker, too, and if Drew gave that a lower rating on the meaningful-life-experience scale, at least her daughter knew now that a royal flush is not what happens when a princess gets embarrassed.

But all that wasn't why Lexi had been so happy. That was because Whit was fun. Drew could see, now, that in her desire to give Lexi's life stability, she had cut off too much spontaneity, and that had been wrong. Whit had shown her that—and he had added some zing to her overly responsible life, as well.

When her dream of being a judge in family court had been impossible, she had become sheriff partly because the job was open, but partly because after a childhood of upheaval, she was comfortable with the straight and narrow. The one time she had strayed from that had been during her love affair with Whit—and look where that had gotten her. So although she could see that it would be good for Lexi if she loosened up a little, she was far from ready to loosen up when it came to whatever was going on between her and Whit.

Whatever it was had made her swallow back a lump in her throat, when she'd seen Whit's proud smile as Lexi had run to them across the soccer field. Whatever it was had made her pulse race when he'd given her a swift, secret kiss just before that three-way hug had ended. Whatever it was had kept Drew up late at night, ever since the night he'd brought her home on his motorcycle, wondering if he would come to her window as he used to do in years past.

But he hadn't, which was just as well, she told herself. Whit might be passing Lexi's prince test, but Drew was still far from ready to try to piece together her old dreams.

When Lexi was finally satisfied with her vantage point, she called her over. They were standing on the sand, looking up at the sky, when Drew heard someone coming down the path. It was Whit. She waved him over to join them.

He pulled her aside. "I couldn't imagine where you were," he said, sounding worried. "What's going on?"

"Not to state the obvious, but we're stargazing," Drew said, feeling a warm rush at his protectiveness. She hadn't been able to tell, the night that tree had gone down, but this time he wasn't bothering to hide the fact that he had been concerned.

"But it's after Lexi's bedtime."

She couldn't resist playing devil's advocate. "Oh, come on, Whit," she argued. "It's Saturday night."

"So? Children find security in—"

"Schedules," she interrupted him, sighing noisily. "I know, I know. But Lexi might sleep in late on the weekends if she stayed up a little later."

He stared at her for a moment and then he caught on. He looked over at Lexi, whose nightgown was billowing in the breeze. "You brought her out here like that?" he said in mock horror. "She doesn't even have any shoes on!"

"It's a beach, Whit."

He made a show of frowning, but Drew could make out a twinkle in his eye. "But she might step on—"

"We're being careful," Drew pointed out.

"And besides, it's *September*. She must be freezing!"

Drew's mouth quirked up at the corner. "I tend not to worry about what the calendar says," she said with a nonchalant shrug. "It was a warm day today."

"And how did she get down that steep path? And in the dark, no less!"

"Princess Lexi rode her royal saddle mare," Drew told him with dignity.

"You mean like this?" he asked, and suddenly swung her onto his back. Drew had to fling her arms around his neck to keep her balance. The laughter they had both been holding back rang out into the night.

Lexi, noticing what was going on, laughed and clapped.

"Bring her over here, Prince Whit," she said. "Did you know I can find the Big Dipper?"

With a flourish, Whit put Drew down on her feet and looked obediently as Lexi pointed up in the sky. Drew smiled as he gave their daughter his full attention, listening carefully as she explained what Drew had just told her. Then he pointed out some other constellations and patiently answered her eager questions about them. As she gazed up at the twinkling sky, trying to listen, Drew found that the most amazing feats of the heroes of Greek mythology couldn't capture her attention more than the simple wonderful feeling of wiggling her bare toes in the September sand.

Much later that night Drew woke from a dreamless sleep into a waking dream, where lines between past

and present merged and blurred. Without seeing anything in the darkness or hearing a sound, she knew
that Whit had come to her.

Conscious thought didn't enter into it as she got
slowly to her feet and walked over to the big window
that faced the ocean. In that dreamy state she stood
in the moonlight that shone into the room, face-to-
face with her old lover, whose moonlit silhouette
waited, silent, behind frames of glass.

She lifted a finger to the windowpane, resting a tip
against the glass. Outside he did the same, joining
their bodies but for the transparent barrier between
them. Slowly she opened her hand and pressed her
palm to the glass, and when he mirrored her gesture
she could almost feel the warmth of his skin against
hers. She pulled her hand away to unlatch the casement, then by slow degrees pushed forward the twin
sashes, gradually opening her bedroom to the murmur
of the ocean and the caress of the breeze and herself
to the power of the man who already held her in
thrall.

She raised her hand again, and this time his palm
met hers without barrier, warm and welcome. When
she offered her other hand, his touch filled that one,
too, and they stood there long moments, face-to-face,
palm to palm, silent, absorbed in the intensity of the
contact. They were looking into each other's eyes, but
seeing far deeper. They were touching each other's
hands, but making a connection that went way beyond
skin-deep.

Still looking into his eyes, she moved her hands to
his shoulders, measuring their breadth, testing the
firmness of the muscles. Again his caress mirrored
hers, and she saw that he was giving her the gift of

control, letting her touch define the parameters of their union. Her fingers trailed down his arms, a whisper of a touch that skimmed the hair that textured them. She felt his involuntary shiver and then became enveloped by her own, as he gave the same light touch back to her.

She reached around him, then, circling him with her arms, massaging his broad back with palms and fingertips, varying the firmness of the pressure as she learned anew the planes of his fully mature body. His hands were warm and strong on her back, kneading and rubbing, ever moving, ever gentle, and she felt a familiar sensation of melting begin in a trickle that, if unchecked, would end in a torrent at her innermost core. The moonlight spilled between them, as their cheeks touched lightly, and she could feel the rub of his rough one against the skin of her smooth one, could hear the rhythm of his breathing, could feel the whisper of his warm breath against the sensitive shell of her ear.

Turning her head, she nuzzled with her lips along his cheek until she found his lips, smoothness over firmness. He joined in her tentative nibbling, testing, teasing, until the trickle inside her gained space and pace with a rush that left her breathless. She sealed the front of their bodies when she sealed their lips, then opened her mouth so that their tongues could meet and entwine, gliding and twirling in a private ritual of ecstasy. Delving her fingers into the long waves of his hair, she put everything she was into that kiss, and was rewarded with the intensity of his response. Moving in this sweet unison, giving was taking, and taking was giving; and with this joining of their bodies she felt her essence blend with his.

It would be easy to be lulled into believing in the enchanting possibility that this could go on forever. But the warm rush inside her was moving ever faster, ever deeper. As inevitable as the pull of the moon on the ocean tides, this kiss was luring them into the need for a deeper connection, a more complete union. When she broke off the kiss, his lips left hers reluctantly, but without pressing her to continue. She took a step backward into her bedroom, and pulled the sashes toward her, closing the casement. As she latched it shut, he put a finger to his lips and pressed it to the window. She did the same, meeting his flesh on the glass, closing her eyes against the well of tears pressing from behind. When she opened them, he was gone.

Back in her bed, drifting from her waking dream back to a dreamless sleep, Drew realized that although her dream castle had fallen down, its foundation was still standing, still solid, still beckoning her to build on it. But now she knew that such a dream couldn't be built by one person alone.

The next morning Drew took Lexi down to Annah's coffee shop for breakfast. Lexi skipped ahead up the steps, yanking the door open with one hand while the other clapped her crown to her head and then disappeared inside.

Drew was anticipating that first cup of coffee, the one that would dispel the cobwebs that were all that was left of the spell she had fallen under last night. She reached for the door handle just as someone pulled it open from inside.

It was Whit. He stood aside, holding the door for her to pass by. She stepped up, and their eyes met;

and in that split second the spell between them was woven once more, beautiful and intact. Then she moved past him, and the spell was broken again. The door closed between them, and then he was gone.

Annah was the only one in the coffee shop. She stood behind the counter, openmouthed, staring at Drew.

Her reaction made Drew uneasy, to say the least. "What?" she said, taking a seat at the empty counter, while the sounds of Lexi playing filtered in from the back room.

Annah leaned on the counter and said, "Do you really want to know what?"

She had that look on her face—the one she wore when her true-love insight blindsided her. Drew had seen it before, but never directed at her. She wished it wasn't now. Not that she wasn't fully prepared to deny it, if Annah told her that she had seen true love between her and Whit. Drew knew better. There was something between them, that was for certain, some deep and elemental attraction. But true love? That was something more, and it seemed to Drew that if she and Whit had it, what had happened seven years ago would have had a different ending.

"No," she said, answering Annah's question. "You might as well save your breath. I have an idea what you're going to say."

Annah grinned knowingly at her. "Your call," she said agreeably. "But just remember, girlfriend. My not saying it doesn't make it any less true."

Into the silence came Lexi, who climbed up on the stool next to Drew.

"What's your pleasure, princess?" Annah asked.

"Milk and a blueberry muffin, please," Lexi said, looking up at her. "And for you to come to my play."

Annah got her order, and coffee and a muffin for Drew. "What play is that?"

"The play I wrote about a princess."

"You wrote a play? All by yourself?"

"Well, I said the words, and my teacher wrote them down. And now my class is going to act it out on back-to-school night, and I get to be the princess," Lexi told her breathlessly. "And there'll be other plays, too, and some band music and singing, and it'll be in the gym in front of everyone, and I want you to come, too. It's next Thursday. Mommy will be there, and Prince Whit, too, of course."

"Of course," Annah echoed, but with a meaningful look at Drew, who did her best to ignore it. She turned back to Lexi. "Not only will I be there, but I'll also let you choose any gown in the back room that you want for your princess costume."

Lexi's eyes shone. "Thanks, Annah!" she said, climbing up to kneel on the counter to hug her. As soon as she finished her breakfast, she flew into the back room to sift through the racks.

Drew went back to join her not long after, while Annah was busy serving a new batch of muffins to a new batch of customers. She heard Lexi's voice as she walked down the hallway. The door to the secondhand shop was open just a crack, enough for Drew to see Lexi looking in the big three-sided mirror, holding a dress to the front of herself. She was talking to the mannequin that stood in the corner.

"No, my dear, not for a ball. It's for a play I'm in," Lexi said. She hesitated, as if listening, and then answered.

"Yes, Annah will be there, and my mommy and—I beg your pardon? My daddy? Well, my daddy is a prince. That is how I got to be a princess, of course."

Drew bit her lip to keep from making a sound as Lexi hung up the dress and got another one. "What?" she asked the mannequin. "Oh, he has a spell cast on him. That's why he left."

Lexi twirled in front of the mirror. "Yes, of course I have a plan. First I have to find him. I decided I would meet as many princes as possible, and then test each one to see if he's the right one." She paused. "No. Prince Erik wasn't the right one, but he did have a spell on him. His heart was frozen. But Julie broke the spell and they fell in love and got married at the castle. And anyway, my real daddy would have to be in love with my *mommy*."

A lump formed in Drew's throat as she listened to her daughter's simple logic. Was Whit in love with her? After last night, she wondered. But she did know that no matter how well matched she and Whit were as lovers, that didn't mean that he would be the best husband for her—or father for Lexi. It put everything in a new perspective, to find out that Lexi was looking not for her prince, but for her daddy. The stakes were much higher now, and Drew knew it.

Lexi put back the second dress and chose another, the pinkest and frilliest one in the shop, dripping with sequins. Drew wondered how she had missed it the first time, because this dress just cried out for a little girl to dress up in it. When she saw herself standing behind it in the mirror, Lexi's green eyes went wide. She didn't say anything for a few minutes, just bounced and twirled, making the dress do the same. Then she spoke again.

"Yes, Prince Whit is doing a good job on the prince daddy tests," she told the mannequin. "But I'm not finished with him yet."

There was a small measure of relief in there for Drew. Maybe she could still help Lexi keep from getting her heart set on Whit, she reasoned, although deep inside she had a hard time believing it.

"When I'm sure I've found my prince daddy, then I have to break the spell," Lexi was saying. "The only problem is, I don't know how to do that yet." She gave one final twirl and then said, with the kind of child's boundless confidence that a parent loved to hear, "But I'm a clever princess, and I'm good at lots of things. I can score goals and send faxes and find constellations, so I guess I can figure out how to break this spell, too. I helped Julie figure out how to break the one on Prince Erik, you know."

She set the dress on the counter next to the register. "I like the one you're wearing, too, but I've decided on this one," she said. "It will be just right for the play, once it's a little shorter."

Then she leaned toward the mannequin, as if listening. "When the spell is finally broken? Why, then he will be my daddy forever, of course, and he'll marry my mommy, and we'll all live happily ever after, because he'll never leave us again."

Drew sagged back against the wall in the hallway. Or else, she thought as her insides caved in, when the spell is broken, Lexi's heart would be too. It was just too much of a stretch for Drew to believe that Whit would never leave them.

Chapter Eight

The last thing Whit wanted to do was leave them. But as he watched Drew's house slip away out of the back window of the limo, he knew that he had no choice.

Lexi's play was that night, and he had been looking forward to going to see it. He was prepared to be proud as any parent had ever been of his kid—after all, she had written it and was playing the lead role. But he knew that even if she just had a walk-on, he would want to be there to see her. He wanted to sit in the audience next to her mother, their arms touching as they sat on the bleachers in the crowded gymnasium. When Lexi came on stage, he and Drew would look at each other and share a secret smile, knowing that they had a part in something really good. Wild horses couldn't have kept him away from Lexi's play.

But a snag in the negotiations he was orchestrating could. The situation had rapidly deteriorated, and now the two countries were making battle noises. In order to avert a crisis, he was jetting to New York to meet their representatives, face-to-face, that very night. This couldn't be put off, even by one hour.

Still, it was the hardest decision Whit had ever made, and facing it had made him feel like a real father. His own disappointment was nothing compared with what Lexi would feel when he wasn't there at the play. He knew she had told all of her classmates that "her" prince was coming to see her in it. Thinking of what she would go through was like taking a solid uppercut right on the chin. He winced, thinking about how she would react, wondering whether she would cry. He wished she had been home now, so that he could tell her himself instead of leaving a note.

And Drew—Drew would be spitting mad. But when he talked to her, she would have to understand. Later, when the veil of secrecy around what he was doing could be safely lifted, he would explain to them why he'd had to leave. Lexi might not understand then, but she would someday, and maybe that would teach her something about responsibility. He was learning more about it every day himself, and one thing he had learned was that he could shoulder far more of it than he had ever thought. And that it felt damn good.

He gave Sloane one last order when they arrived at the airport, before striding briskly off across the tarmac to where his private jet sat waiting. He carried his briefcase in one hand, his overnight bag in the other and the unaccustomed weight of the world on his shoulders.

"He never came, did he, Mommy?"

Drew looked down at her daughter's wide, sad eyes

and trembling mouth. She shook her head. "He said he wouldn't be able to in his note. Remember, honey?"

"I just thought he might finish his urnjit business fast and be able to come after all," Lexi said disappointedly.

Disappointment was far too mild a reaction for Drew. She didn't know what "urnjit" business a man who didn't have an official assignment from the king could have, but he had *no* business making a promise to Lexi and then not following through. Not that Drew shouldn't have been expecting it. She could kick herself for not preparing Lexi for the possibility, and the fact that she didn't showed how thoroughly she had been taken in over the past weeks by Whit's...well, by *Whit*.

"I thought the play was wonderful, Lexi," she told her daughter. "You remembered all your lines and made a very enchanting princess. Annah loved it, too. She's waiting for us outside. Let's go, honey."

It was getting late, and snuggling into bed might be the best antidote for Lexi's letdown. Hers, too. In the morning they could have a serious talk about promises and trust. And if she could have spared Lexi the hurt, Drew would have said that a healthy dose of disillusionment was not an altogether bad thing for her daughter to experience, where a certain prince was concerned. Today, a missed play; tomorrow, who knew what?

Drew steered Lexi through the backstage crowd and out of the side door of the gym. Annah joined them and gave Lexi such heartfelt congratulations with her hug that Lexi gave her a wobbly smile. They started for the car, when something at the end of the sidewalk caught their eye. It was Whit's limo, parked under a streetlight, with a small, curious crowd gathered around it.

Sloane, standing at attention beside it, beckoned to Lexi, who instantly perked up and pulled Drew along with her to the limo. Drew, after rolling her eyes at Annah, went along only because she had no choice.

When they reached the limo, Sloane opened the back door with a flourish. "His Highness, Prince Whit of Isle Anders has sent me to provide transportation home for Princess Lexi," he announced. "And to present her with these, after her performance." To the crowd's oohs and aahs, he handed Lexi a bouquet of pink sweetheart roses and then opened the door of the limo for her.

Lexi got in, a radiant smile lighting her face. Out of the window she waved to the crowd, which, Drew noticed, included some of the classmates who had scoffed earlier in the week when Lexi had told them that "her prince" was going to come to see her in the play.

Because it would have made a bigger fuss if she had refused, Drew let Sloane hand her into the limo next. She was glad to see a smile on her daughter's face. And though Whit's doing had put it there, she needed no reminder that his doing had also taken it away in the first place.

As Lexi's prince, he had pulled through. But as her father...that was an entirely different matter. Drew doubted that some flowers and a limo ride would cut it, even with her starry-eyed daughter.

But Drew had overestimated Lexi's disappointment, or underestimated her attachment to Whit. That

night and the next day and the next, Lexi staunchly
defended him, saying that she knew he had important
work to do, but that didn't mean he didn't *want* to
see her play. She trusted him unconditionally, forgave
him absolutely and looked forward to seeing him
again eagerly.

He was supposed to pick her up that very afternoon
for soccer. When Drew dropped her off at Annah's
on the way to her final Saturday meeting before next
week's retreat, she warned Lexi over and over that
she doubted Whit would show up. There had been no
sign of him for the past two days. But Lexi waved
goodbye from the top of Annah's steps, confident that
since her prince hadn't sent word telling her that she
wasn't coming, then he definitely was.

Drew drove away not knowing whether it would
be better for Lexi if he didn't show up, or if he did.
She did know why she had been more critical of his
no-show at the play—princes could get away with
that kind of thing, but not dads. And not the man who
had left Drew alone, when she had been counting on
him. Lexi had escaped major hurt this time, but it just
sealed Drew's opinion that it would be better for her
to have no father at all than one who might disappear
into thin air just when she needed him most.

Whit saw Drew sitting on the front porch swing
reading the newspaper, when he brought Lexi home
from soccer. He had seen her car drive past the field
after her meeting, but this time she hadn't stopped.
And he was pretty sure he knew why.

Lexi ran ahead, stopping to kiss her mother before
disappearing in the house to fix her crown, which had
fallen off and been stepped on during the final scrim-

mage. Whit walked alone up the steps to the porch, where Drew's silence greeted him.

Better than a whack over the head with the newspaper, he told himself. "Hello, Drew," he said out loud.

She dropped the paper to her lap and looked up at him, but said nothing.

"I'm sorry about missing the play," he began.

"You should tell Lexi that," she said. "Hers is the heart that you broke."

This time. She didn't say the words, but still, they seemed to echo in the air around them.

"I already talked to Lexi. She was remarkably understanding."

"Maybe you should tell me whatever magic words you told her, Your Highness," Drew said, crossing her arms. "Then maybe I can be understanding, too."

Without being invited, he sat down on the swing next to her. "I can't tell you much," he said. "I'm involved in some volatile negotiations at a high-security level."

"I thought the king hadn't given you a new assignment."

"He hasn't. I got into this on my own."

"It doesn't involve Isle Anders?"

"Not directly. But it's a matter of international interest."

She dropped her eyes to the newspaper, and he saw a picture of himself standing face-to-face with a gorgeous blonde in a low-cut gown, a bouquet of flowers clasped between their intertwined hands. It had been taken on the steps of the hotel as he was leaving. She had dropped the flowers, and he was handing them to her. He had never seen the woman before. But the photo made it look like a matter of *personal* interest.

He groaned, wondering when, if ever, he would be able to live down his reputation. He couldn't blame Drew if she thought the worst. "You don't really—" he began.

"Care?" she finished casually, tossing the paper aside. "Not in the least. Except about how all this affects Lexi."

She didn't care about him, about *them?* He pushed the thought aside for the moment. "Lexi understands," he said pointedly.

"Lexi was dazzled by the princely amends you made after missing her play," Drew corrected.

"I *wanted* to go. My not being there couldn't be helped," he said in frustration. "I left word ahead of time and tried to make things better afterward. I did my best, Drew."

"As a *prince*," Drew conceded. "But what about as a—"

Just then Lexi stepped out onto the porch. The silence hung thick with unspoken accusations that even a six-year-old couldn't miss. She eyed them curiously. "Are you two having an argument?"

"Yes." Drew said it at the same time Whit did. Apparently they agreed on that, he thought, and on the importance of being honest with their daughter.

Surprisingly, Lexi's reaction was a broad smile. "I thought so," she said, and skipped back inside the house.

Mystified at her behavior, Whit turned to Drew. "Do you know what that was all about?"

"I have an idea," Drew mumbled, but didn't elaborate. Instead, she stood and gathered up the scattered newspaper to take inside. At the doorway she looked back at Whit. "I think you'd better go now," she said, too softly for Lexi to hear, even if she was right inside listening.

But Lexi, apparently, had radar. She came barreling around from the backyard and stood in Whit's path as he went to his car. "Prince Whit, you can't leave now!" she said. "What about the tape?"

"What tape?" Drew asked.

"Prince Whit had Mr. Sloane make a videotape of my play so that he could see it when he got back," Lexi answered her. "He has it in the car, and he said we could watch it with him. Can we, Mommy?"

"Maybe another day," Drew said. "This just isn't a good time."

"Because you and Prince Whit are having an argument?" Lexi asked, wide-eyed.

Because she was so mixed up, she didn't want to be around Prince Whit, Drew thought desperately. She was angry at him for missing the play, but she felt sorry for him, too, because he had missed it. It made no sense. The offbeat things he did with Lexi drove her crazy, but his growing devotion to her daughter touched Drew in ways that were wonderfully new. How was she supposed to know whether or not he'd be a good father, when he didn't do the same thing two days in a row?

And then there was the two of them. His actions toward her had made it clear that he wanted to be her lover again, but his restraint in letting her determine that part of their relationship betrayed that she meant even more to him. She should be jealous, seeing the picture of him with that woman, but the thought hadn't crossed her mind, except to bait him. What was wrong with her? Was she crazy to trust him, or crazy not to?

Lexi was still looking up at her, waiting for an answer. She knew why her daughter was so happy that she and Whit were arguing. Strangers were distantly polite; people who cared about each other cared enough to air their disagreements. Parents of her friends argued, and then made up. Well, if Lexi was looking for that, or for more arguing, she was going to be disappointed. Tonight, and until she made up her mind, Drew would be distantly polite.

"Prince Whit and I aren't arguing anymore," she told Lexi. "But this might not be a good time for him, because he just got back from his trip."

Lexi turned to Whit, expectantly.

"Let's see," he mused. "Which would I rather do—unpack or see Lexi in her play?" He held his hands out in front of him as a scale on which to weigh the relative merits of each. "Unpack. Play. Unpack. Play."

Lexi saw right through his teasing. She took both his hands in hers and hauled him to his car. "See the play and unpack later!" she said, grinning.

He pulled the tape out of the glove box and held it up, looking at Drew questioningly. She nodded, and they all went in the house.

They watched it three times through, all of it. Lexi told what it was like to be backstage, and Drew, what it was like to be in the audience. She kept her explanation on the dry side, remembering her promise to herself to be distantly polite. But Whit's curious enthusiasm proved to be infectious, and before she knew it, they were all laughing as they sat on the floor of the living room, a bowl of popcorn between them, using the remote to look at the play fast forward, backward and slow motion, and to pause the tape at the place where Princess Lexi peeked through the stage curtain to wave her scepter at Sloane.

By then it was late and they were hungry, so Drew ordered out for pizza—delivered!—which they ate while watching a videotape of Lexi's kindergarten class.

"Do you have any other tapes of her?" Whit asked when it was over. He was hungry for glimpses into his daughter's past.

Drew shook her head. "I only have this one because the father of one of her classmates took it to give to the teacher at the end of the year, and he made copies for anyone who gave him a blank."

"We can't afford a video camera," Lexi explained to him. "But we have a *regular* camera. Mommy took lots of pictures of me, when I was little. Do you want to see some?"

"Do I!" He sat on the sofa with Lexi curled up next to him, paging through photo albums, starting with the most recent. Drew had declined his offer to help clean up. When she was finished in the kitchen, she wandered back into the living room and sat perched on the arm of the sofa next to him. Lexi gave most of the explanations, but as they worked their way backward in time, Drew had to fill in more and more. Whit liked the way she remembered details about the things they had done when Lexi was younger and shared even the most seemingly trivial with him. He wanted to know it all, to feel it all— wanted desperately to have been a part of it all.

"That was the time I gave her her first haircut,"

Drew said, pointing to a picture of Lexi sitting in her high chair with a big sheet draped around her.

"How old was she?"

"Two. She was a little baldie when she was born, so it took until then for her bangs to grow long enough to get into her eyes. That's when I decided it was time for a trim. See," she said, reaching across him to point. "Here's the before, and here's the after."

He was momentarily distracted by having her arm, so slender and feminine, right in front of his chest. She smelled good, too, and he wondered what she would do if he pulled her down onto his lap and trailed kisses up that arm, from the tips of her fingers to the crown of her shoulder. But Lexi was there, sitting right next to him, and that gave him pause. Respectable fathers no doubt didn't do such things. Instead, he let his gaze trail down the length of Drew's gracefully pointing finger and looked at the pictures.

"I notice you didn't cut the rest of her hair," he observed.

"Cut off those curls? Not a chance!" Drew said, smiling. She liked the way he was truly interested in looking at these. No one else was, except maybe Julie and Annah. Poor Lexi not only didn't have a father, she didn't have grandparents to fuss over her, either.

Like King Ivar had fussed over her at Julie and Erik's wedding. They had taken a shine to each other immediately. If Lexi gained Whit as a father, she'd be getting a grandfather, too, and an uncle. She had won Erik over when he'd stayed there at the castle that summer.

Right here, right now, Whit was acting like a father, Drew had to admit. No, not acting; his interest wasn't feigned. He wanted to be here, doing this. He wanted to know everything about his daughter. And he had wanted to be at the play.

"Your hair is sure a lot longer now," he said to Lexi. "Maybe we should give you another haircut, and cut off those curls this time." When she didn't respond to his teasing, he looked down at her. She was sound asleep.

He got up and gently picked her up in his arms. "I can do that," Drew said, getting to her feet, too.

"Maybe, but I'm not going to let you," he growled. He'd never done this before. Besides, he knew full well that this was something that dads were supposed to do. And Drew was still so petite and fragile looking, despite her toughness, that he wondered she could carry Lexi around at all. "She's mine tonight."

He carried her upstairs and tucked her into bed, clothes and all. Drew watched with a lump in her throat as he gave her a gentle kiss on the forehead, then stepped aside so that she could do the same. They stood side by side by the light of the night-light, watching their daughter sleep, her face smooth and untroubled, her breathing steady and deep, before closing the door behind them and going downstairs.

Whit went immediately back to the photo album they had set aside and found the spot where they'd left off. Drew hadn't asked him to stay, but she hadn't told him to leave, either, and that was invitation enough for him.

Drew couldn't think of a good enough reason to kick him out, so she poured each of them another glass of the red wine they'd shared with the pizza and sat down on the other side of the sofa. Whit was truly

enthralled with the pictures of Lexi as a toddler, and
that was hard for her to resist. He asked her endless
questions—what their days were like, how long Lexi
napped, what she liked to eat.

"I'll bet she was smart," he said, looking at a picture of Lexi, wearing nothing but a diaper and little
blue sneakers too tiny to be true, scribbling with chalk
on the driveway.

"As a whip," Drew told him proudly, tucking her
bare feet up under her. "She was talking in sentences
by her first birthday and reciting nursery rhymes not
long after that." It didn't seem like bragging, saying
it to Whit. And it was a relief to be able to share her
full measure of pride in her daughter with the only
other person who could feel it as strongly. It might
have been the wine mellowing her, but Drew also felt
like she could share riskier things with Whit, too—
like her hopes for Lexi, and a parent's deepest fears.

By the time they got to Lexi's newborn pictures,
Drew found she had inched across the sofa until she
was sitting right next to Whit. She hadn't realized it,
because she had become as caught up as he was in
experiencing the past. She noticed it now, but what
she noticed was that it felt comfortable.

Whit was aware right away that Drew was drawing
nearer to him, inch by agonizingly slow inch, and that
made him less and less comfortable. While his conscious attention never strayed from the photo album,
every male fiber of his being went on full alert. Twice
he had to stop himself from reflexively putting his
arm around her to pull her right next to him, squelch-
ing the outraged masculine instincts that were telling
him loud and clear that that was where she belonged.

But when he saw the first picture ever taken of

Lexi, just minutes after she was born, instinct and emotion combined to overwhelm him. He pulled Drew into his arms and held on tight, burying his face against her neck.

His reaction left her breathless. He was genuinely choked up, and that moved her almost to tears. Instinctively wanting to help soften the hard edges of his emotion, she reached over to turn off the lamp by the sofa, leaving them in the muted light from the kitchen. She rubbed her hands along his back, letting him take whatever it was he needed from her.

"I wish I had been there when she was born," he said finally in a husky whisper right against her neck.

Sensing that he needed to talk this through, she asked, "What would you have done?"

"I would have gathered her into my arms," he said softly, gathering Drew more closely, as if to demonstrate.

"And then what?" she prompted, loving the feel of his strength surrounding her.

"And then I would have brought her to her mother."

Caught by surprise, Drew felt a strangled sob escape her. While she sought control, he went on.

"And while you held our baby for the first time, I would have sat down beside you with my arms around you, like this," he said, shifting her slightly so he could show her. "And I would have thanked you over and over again for having given me the most precious gift a woman can give a man."

"The baby?" she choked out.

"Babies are a gift from God," he said softly. "The gift you gave me was your love."

At his words, tears overflowed her eyes. She let

them fall, one by one, onto his shoulder as she clung to him. "I...I never told you that," she whispered into his ear.

"You didn't have to," he said. "I knew."

"How?"

"Your eyes told me when you looked at me. Your lips told me when you smiled at me." His voice was husky in the semidarkness. "Your body told me when you gave yourself to me."

Heaven help her, he was right, so right. She wondered what her body was telling him now, as she bathed in his warmth and closeness.

"You're not a woman who would sleep with a man you didn't love. I know I was your first," he murmured. "All these years, I've wondered if I was the only—"

She put a finger to his lips to hush him. Looking right into his eyes, she nodded. There was no need to keep secret from him something that she had probably already told him, on some level.

He kissed her finger, then took her hand in his. "I'm glad our baby was conceived in love."

It was the closest he had ever come to telling her that he had loved her, too, back then, and Drew felt as though she had been given a priceless gift. "If you only knew how many times I had thought of that," she said. It had been something to hang on to, during the rough times.

"Do you know when it happened?"

"Yes."

"It was that last night, wasn't it?"

"Yes."

And then he had left. But if he'd known then what he knew now...

He looked into her green eyes, which were soft with memories. "What was it like, at first?" he asked, toying with her fingers on the hand he still held.

She bit her lip. "Scary," she said, then corrected herself. "No. Terrifying." A faint smile played around her lips. "But wonderful, too."

He was still focused on scary. "Was your grandmother rough on you?"

"She died before I told her. But that was part of what made it so scary. She would have been furious, but without her, I was so *alone*."

"Was there talk, here in town?"

"I'm sure there was," she said with a shrug. "But I kept to myself, for the most part. I was working and going to the community college, and most of my friends from high school were off somewhere doing one thing or another. Julie, too."

"Is that when you met Annah? At your doctor's office, right?"

She nodded. "We really connected. It was great to have someone there with me when I needed it. But she was still married then, and..."

Her voice trailed off, telling him that, for the most part, she had gone through pregnancy alone. And scared. And hurt by his leaving, and too proud to ask for help of any kind from him, after his desertion. If he had known then...

He tightened his arms, giving her a reassuring squeeze. "Tell me about the wonderful part."

"The wonderful part was being pregnant. Don't get me wrong," she added quickly. "It was plenty uncomfortable at times. But to know there's a baby growing inside you... It's amazing."

He put his hand on her belly. "Right here?"

She blushed, then grinned. "Where else, you idiot?"

"It's just so flat now, like it was before. It's hard to believe Lexi was in there." There was awe in his voice, and his fingers were warm as they stole under her clothes and rested right against her skin. "I would have put my hand right here and felt her move."

"Mmm." He was stroking her now, his hand flat against her smooth skin. Her insides began to hum in a sensuous prelude.

"I would have rubbed your aches and pains away," he murmured, running his hands down her legs now. "Massaged your feet, at the end of a long day." He cradled her foot in his big, warm hand, and the pressure he applied made her relax in his arms.

"I would have soothed your tired muscles," he went on, dragging his hands back up her legs, lingeringly. She wondered if she had ever felt so cherished. His touch was tender and warm. It was comforting, and it was exciting. It brought the womanly part of her slowly to life. "From head to toe, especially here," he whispered, moving his hands around to her back, underneath her shirt, kneading rhythmically as she closed her eyes and let her head drop back.

His kiss swallowed up her moan of pleasure. It was a full, lusty kiss, devoid of preliminaries. His lips breached hers and opened them, his tongue found its mate, and she gave herself wholly over to the tantalizing invasion of her senses. She was full to the brim, and aching to be filled. She was at the height of pleasure, yet knowing there were greater heights beyond. When his hand returned to her belly, she felt an explosion of warmth underneath it.

His brain cautioned him to slow down, but that was

about as useless as trying to shout across the ocean to Isle Anders. He was wrapped up in the feel of her, her smell, her taste. He deepened the kiss, and still she demanded more of him. It had always been like that. They never could get enough of each other, and he hadn't had nearly enough for now. He slid his hand up over her ribs and cupped one breast. It was fuller than before, and he gloried in the weight of it in his hand.

Just then a cry came from upstairs. They both sat bolt upright on the sofa, untangling themselves.

"Mommy!" Lexi called again, fretfully.

Drew stood up, pulling her shirt down, then hurried up the stairs. Whit stood up, too, but he stayed downstairs, wandering around the living room as he regained some semblance of control. Minutes later, Drew came back down.

"Is she all right?"

She nodded. "I don't think she was fully awake. She was looking for her frog, which wasn't in her bed when we tucked her in. Once she had it in her arms, she dropped right back to sleep."

But Whit knew that Lexi's awakening had changed things between him and Drew. It wasn't just that the mood was spoiled: her making her presence known had brought them back to reality, back to the present. It had rooted their passion and given it a context.

Drew took a deep breath. "Things...ah, got a little out of hand," she said quietly, blamelessly.

Whit nodded his agreement. There was regret tangled up in the awkwardness of the moment—but it was regret both at what they'd done, and what they hadn't gotten to do. He hoped she saw that, too.

"That doesn't mean it was a mistake, Drew," he said. "We both saw this coming for a long time."

She didn't deny it, but she crossed her arms protectively, looking small and alone as she stood across the room from him. "I think it's a good thing she woke up when she did."

He walked slowly up to her, then, around the sofa to where she stood by the front door, his eyes never breaking contact with hers. "It doesn't change the fact that you want me as much as I want you."

Drew was silent for a moment, trying to conjure up the words that would make him understand. "Whit, I was your lover once, but I can't be your lover again. It's just not enough," she said softly. "I want you, but I need more."

Chapter Nine

"Are you sure you want to get married?" Drew asked.

She pushed her lunch aside and looked across her desk at the young woman who had just come into her office. It was Jamie Sloane, the youngest of Gary's five older sisters, which meant she was only twenty or so.

"Very sure," Jamie answered.

"Here?"

"Right here."

"You don't want to have a more traditional wedding? Or at least have the ceremony somewhere where your family will fit more comfortably?" Drew asked, scanning her tiny office.

The girl rolled her eyes. "With the size of my family, it would take too long to get them all together. Eloping is much more convenient, believe me. I'll tell them all about it tomorrow, after the wedding night."

Drew felt her jaw drop. "Are you saying you want to do this *now*?"

"Right now." Jamie leaned forward as if telling her best friend a secret, which made her seem even younger to Drew. "You see, Sheriff Davis, I'm going to have a baby. So I don't want to wait."

Time spun backward for Drew, to when she herself was young, single and pregnant. Her life had turned out fine, but she remembered how it felt, then, to face an uncertain future, alone.

Her thoughts were interrupted by Jamie, who seemed barely able to contain her excitement. "Look. I've got all the papers right here," she said eagerly, handing them over to Drew. "Can you do it?"

Of course Drew was capable of performing a legal wedding. No one had ever called on her to do it yet, but there was a first time for everything. "I could do it," she said, riffling through the paperwork, "but there's one thing missing."

Jamie's face fell. "What's that?"

"A groom."

"Oh, is that all?" Jamie said, with a relieved laugh. "I've got one of them. He'll be along any minute, as soon as his shift is over at the processing plant. It's Josh Cranson. You know him, don't you, Sheriff?"

Drew did. He was a pal of Jamie's brother Gary, young and handsome. Between them they'd broken the heart of every young girl in town. Neither one was within shouting distance of what Drew would call husband material.

"Since you want me to perform the ceremony, Jamie, I have to ask you something," she said.

"What is it?"

"Are you marrying Josh because you think it's your only option?"

"Oh, gosh, not at all, Sheriff Davis! Did I make it seem that way?" Jamie said. "Josh asked me to marry him last spring. The baby is just hurrying things along is all." She smiled. "And just between us girls, if I'd had my way, Josh and I would have been married the day after he asked me. I've been in love with him since the days I used to tag along after him and Gary."

"Okay, Jamie," Drew said. "But just so you know, I'm going to ask him the same thing, when he gets here. If I'm going to marry you, I've got to be sure it's what you both want."

"I know how we can speed things up," Jamie said confidently. "May I make a call?"

Assuming she was going to try to track Josh down, Drew pointed to the phone on her desk. But Jamie called someone else.

"Annah?" she said. "Hi, it's Jamie Sloane. Listen, we're going to go through with it. Yep. I'm in Sheriff Davis's office right now. Would you talk to her for me?"

Drew took the phone. "Hi, Annah."

There was a smile in Annah's voice. "So you're going to perform your first wedding."

"Assuming the groom shows up," Drew said dryly. "And assuming that you give this union your blessing."

Annah laughed. "I've seen this one coming for years," she said. "Josh was a moving target for a while, but Cupid's arrow hit him all the same. You can marry those two without compunction, girlfriend. It's true love, all right."

Drew hung up the phone, wondering why true love was enough for some couples. It didn't seem to be for her and Whit. She hadn't seen him since Saturday night, although she knew he had been at the Point the whole time. That night she had taken a stand—and he had backed off. She had no idea what he was thinking, or when she would see him again.

She shared her lunch with Jamie and then went back to work. Every once in a while she glanced up and watched the bride-to-be leafing through a magazine. Jamie was excited, but not nervous. He was already over an hour late for their wedding, but she was confident her groom was going to be there.

True love didn't let her down. Josh showed up not long after one o'clock, with a heartfelt apology, a passionate kiss and a golden wedding band that he'd been waiting for the jeweler to inscribe.

"We're all ready," Jamie said breathlessly, when the kiss was over. "Hitch us up, Sheriff."

"Where's your witness?" Drew asked.

Jamie turned to Josh. "Where's Gary?"

"Isn't he here?"

"No. When you were late, I assumed he was with you." For the first time, Jamie looked flustered. She called the castle for her brother, but there was no answer. "That rat," she said, hanging up the phone. "We'll never be able to find him."

"Do you mind using someone else?" Drew asked.

"No. We'll take anyone," Jamie said.

Drew picked up the phone and called Annah, but the line was busy. She tried twice more, but it was the same. Josh was about to charge outside to pull someone in off the street when there was a knock on Drew's office door.

It was Whit. Drew's reaction when he walked in the door was so strong she knew it was from more than just the unexpectedness of seeing him. She had to consciously hang on to the arms of her chair to keep from being physically propelled forward into his arms by a force she didn't understand.

Jamie ran over to him instead. "Is Gary parking the limo?"

Whit dragged his eyes from Drew to give her a look of mild puzzlement. "No. I rode my cycle here."

"Where is he?"

"Apparently he was out late last night," Whit said with a shrug. "As far as I know, he's still in bed."

Josh was pacing around the room, muttering, "I'll kill him, I'll kill him," while he pounded his fist into his palm.

"Why didn't you wake him up?" Jamie asked Whit sharply.

"I didn't need him," Whit said, giving her a curious look. "But you obviously do."

Jamie colored, apparently realizing how she had been speaking to Whit. "Oh, I beg your pardon, Your Highness. I'm his sister, Jamie. He was supposed to meet me here at noon, to get married."

"I didn't realize things were quite so backward here," Whit said dryly.

Jamie put a hand to her mouth, in horror. "No, no," she said, with a nervous laugh. "I'm not marrying *Gary*. Sheriff Davis is marrying me and Josh. Oh, shoot. That doesn't sound right, either."

Drew stood up. "Jamie and Josh are getting married, I'm performing the ceremony, and Gary was supposed to be the witness," she clarified.

"Since he's not here, will you do it, Your Highness?" Jamie asked him. "I'm sure it won't take long."

"It would be an honor," he told her gravely, and then looked at Drew.

Her heart took a leap as their eyes met. And then it began to pound. Performing this wedding ceremony took on an added dimension, with Whit in the room. She glanced over at Jamie and Josh, who were looking at her expectantly. "Are you two ready?" she asked. They nodded.

"Then let's get started." She walked over to the lone window in her office, which overlooked the town common. All was quiet in the early afternoon, but it was pretty out there, with the trees tinged with color. She stood with her back to the window and arranged the three of them facing her.

"Jamie asked me to say a few words, before we get on to the ceremony itself," she began. "I'm not a preacher, and I'm not a judge, but I am honored to share with you whatever wisdom I might have. Which just about guarantees this will be short."

They all laughed, and that relaxed Drew a bit, as much as she could relax with three pairs of eyes fixed on her, one of them Whit's blue ones, which had had the power at various times to mesmerize, reassure, tease and impassion her. She cleared her throat and started.

"Sometimes people know right from the beginning when they find the one for them," she said. "It was like that for you, Jamie and Josh. It's a special feeling, isn't it? Like heaven is smiling down on the two of you."

They exchanged besotted grins, their hands intertwined.

"But when things start out like that, so blessed and wonderful," Drew went on, feeling Whit's steady gaze, "it can be the toughest way to begin a relationship. Things move fast, because it feels so right. You take for granted that the road you're traveling will stay that smooth and open."

She took a deep breath and gave them a small smile. "But it won't, Jamie and Josh. That's nothing against either of you, or what you feel for each other. It's just the way of the world. As sure as the leaves are going to fall off those trees out on the common, the road you're on is going to get rough. There's a bumpy patch waiting for you less than nine months along when your baby arrives, an awesome blessing and an unbelievable challenge all in one. Count on it, there'll be even rougher patches along that road. And not only that, sometimes it'll curve around so much that you won't be sure where you're heading. Sometimes it will get so obscure you won't even be sure you're still on it. And there's going to be more than one fork in it, I'll guarantee you that."

She paused. They were all listening intently, eyes glued on her. "But if you keep holding on to each other, the way you are right now, you'll stay on that road, one way or another. And I think the way things turn out, you find that the important thing isn't staying on the road, after all," she said softly. "It's just being together."

When she stopped, Jamie was crying. While Josh got a tissue from the desk to wipe her tears away, Drew looked at Whit.

It had finally happened. She had fallen in love with

him all over again, or maybe she had never stopped loving him. All she knew was that because of him, she was daring to dream again, and once more she was asking him to share that dream. She didn't know what his answer would be, but she did know that it was time to put their love to the test. Seven years ago, when they had stood at this place in the road, they had each taken a different fork; but now their paths had intertwined again. She wondered where they would go from here: whether they would start out together this time, step by step toward a future together, or whether they would go off on separate, lonely paths again.

When the bride and groom were ready, Drew had them repeat their wedding vows. They were the traditional ones passed down from time out of mind. Whit had heard them countless times before, but never out of Drew's lips. This time, those ancient vows took on new meaning.

Do you take this woman...to have and to hold...to love, honor and cherish...forsaking all others...as long as you both shall live?

After the vows were spoken, there was a long silence while the bride and groom kissed. He and Drew exchanged looks. Her expression was soft, but not yielding. Waiting, but not expectant. At peace, but not contented. That's when he knew that where they went from here was in his hands. Last time they were together, she had said that she needed more; today, she had defined her terms. It was up to him to accept them, if he so chose. To prove that he could live up to those sacred vows. To convince her that he would stay with her, no matter how long, rough, twisting or obscure their road became. To walk the walk.

But first he would have to lay to rest his old nemesis. The more he wanted to make Drew's dreams come true, the closer his old fear of failure loomed in the background.

With the wedding ceremony over, all that was left was the paperwork. Whit signed where he was supposed to and waited while the newlyweds thanked Drew. When the office door closed behind them, silence descended.

"Well done," he said, filling the void.

She seemed grateful. "Thank you. I was... nervous." He thought she was going to say something else, but her tone turned businesslike. "What can I do for you?"

He had almost forgotten why he'd come to her office in the first place. He picked up a large envelope from the corner of her desk, where he'd set it down. "I need to have my signature notarized," he said. "I understand you can do that."

"Yes. I'm a notary public, too."

"Jack of all trades?"

"Look who's talking," she said. "Is this part of that secret business you've been involved in?"

"Yes," Whit said, and there was pride in his voice. His first draft of the agreement had been well received. They had hammered out a few changes over the phone, and now he was sending both parties a copy of what could be the final agreement. With the exception of one bone of contention that they would have to compromise on, Whit had engineered it so that they both pretty much got what they wanted. He felt he had reason to be proud.

Drew got out her seal and notarized both copies of the document. "All set," she said, handing the envelope back to him. They sat across the desk from each other, neither sure what to say next.

The ringing of the phone settled it. Drew answered, and Whit saw her frown.

"What's wrong? Oh, that's too bad."

Whit watched as she bit her lip in concern. "So she's all right? How long?" She paused. "Well, of course you should. What about work, though?"

She shifted the phone to her other ear. "Oh, that's fine, then. What? Don't you *dare* worry about that! Being with your mother is much more important. Go. I'll keep an eye on the place while you're gone. Have a safe trip. 'Bye."

She hung up the phone. "That was Annah," she told him. "Her mother fell and broke her leg in two places. She's going home to Indiana, to help out for a little while. She's leaving now."

Whit figured out what Drew had told Annah not to worry about. "What about your retreat? You've been planning it for weeks."

Drew shrugged. "Family comes first," she said, and he knew she meant Annah's family as well as her own.

"But Drew, you organized this. This thing is your baby."

"*Lexi* is my baby. Three days is a long time for her to stay even with a good friend," she said. "No. I wouldn't consider asking anyone else in town."

There was a pause before Whit spoke again. "What about someone at the castle?"

"We'll put the girls over here and the boys over there."

Whit looked at the pile of "guests" for the masquerade ball Lexi was staging in the castle ballroom, wondering how in the world he was supposed to tell a girl stuffed animal from a boy stuffed animal. Watching Lexi, he got the feeling it had something to do with the color of the bows around their necks, so he gamely pitched in and helped separate the furry pile by gender—with only a few mistakes, which Lexi found uproariously funny.

That was how taking care of Lexi while Drew was away was going to be, he thought. A couple of months ago this would have been completely foreign to his experience, but by now he had spent mornings, afternoons and evenings with Lexi—just not for three days in a row. But he was more than game to give this a try, and overall he thought he was doing okay. It was already Saturday morning. Drew had left twenty-four hours earlier and would be back on Sunday night.

Her agreeing to let him do this, he saw as a tremendous show of faith. It made him want to prove to her—and to himself—that she could trust him to be a good father for Lexi. It was all the chance he could want, to show her that he had changed; that she could depend on him; that he wouldn't run scared from her love or from the responsibility of being a husband and father. Those might be her terms, but hell, they were his terms, too. He didn't want anything else but to be in tight with her and Lexi, and give them all the love he had in his heart for them. He wanted the three of them to be a real family. He only hoped that his desire was strong enough to put his doubts to rest.

He was feeling good about how he was carving out a role for himself as a prince. Since the negotiations he had mediated had gone well, it looked as if he had found a way that he could use his people skills and turn the unconventional way he looked at the world from a drawback to an asset. All he was waiting for was for both countries to sign off on the final version of the agreement. When that happened, he would talk to his father about his future as a member of the ruling family—he was tired of bouncing around from task to task, and was ready to make his mark on Isle Anders and on the world.

Down the hall the phone rang. Lexi looked up from where she sat knotting Whit's silk handkerchiefs around the "girls" for dresses. "Maybe it's Mommy," she said.

"No, princess," he told her. "Remember your mommy said that there wouldn't be a phone available at the retreat, except for emergencies?"

"Yes, but why?"

"That's what a retreat is all about," he explained patiently. "It's so—"

Just then, Sloane appeared in the doorway of the ballroom. "You're wanted on the phone," he told Whit. "I think you'll want to take this one in the library," he added, glancing over at Lexi. "It sounds like trouble."

It was trouble, all right. An unforeseen complication was threatening to blow apart the negotiations he had engineered. The situation was extremely volatile. The representatives of both countries were asking him to come back to New York for another face-to-face meeting, which they saw as the only way to avert a crisis.

He spent ten more minutes looking at the problem from every direction, but they were right. He had no choice but to get to New York, and fast. He got both parties to agree to a meeting time and place, and was about to get Sloane to make some quick travel arrangements while he packed, when he thought of something.

"Lexi!" he said out loud in the empty room.

"Here I am, Prince Whit!" she said, jumping out from behind a chair.

Good thing he had a strong heart. She had sure taken him by surprise. "Lexi, I thought you were in the ballroom."

"I was, but I thought you might be lonely, so I came in here."

"Did you hear me talking?" he asked, coming around the desk and squatting down next to her.

She started to shake her head, but he gave her a penetrating look, and she changed it to a nod. "Are you really going away?" she whispered.

"I have to," he said.

"What about me?" she asked.

What about her, indeed? Drew was virtually unreachable, especially in the short amount of time he had; Annah was still away; and Drew had made it clear that she didn't trust anyone else to take care of Lexi.

Except him. She had trusted him, and that meant there was only one answer to Lexi's question. "Why, you're going with me, of course," he said.

Her face lit up. "To New York?"

"Yes."

"Is Mr. Sloane going to drive us?"

"He's going to drive us to the airport."

Her eyes widened. "We're going to ride in a plane?"

"Yes," Whit said. "Listen, princess, I need you to

pack up your bag while I talk to Mr. Sloane and get a few things ready. Can you do that?''

''Yes, and can I bring all my stuffed animals on the plane? They've never ridden on one, either.''

''Every one,'' Whit said. No doubt passengers like that would be a first for his pilot, but hey, whatever it took.

''And my fancy dresses?''

''Absolutely.''

Lexi threw herself into his arms. ''Thank you, Prince Whit,'' she said. ''This is just what a princess's special prince would do.''

Whit was so pumped up he thought he would burst. Not only was he was doing what Drew would expect of him, but he was also passing Lexi's prince test. Oh, yeah. He was going to stop a war from starting, all right. No *sweat*. He might also fly alongside the plane to New York and leap the Empire State Building, while he was at it. And when he got home, he was going to move his women into his castle, so that they could all start living happily ever after.

''Ready to get started, princess?''

''Ready,'' she said. ''But shouldn't we call Mommy?''

He thought about that. He could leave a message for Drew in an emergency, but he didn't think this qualified as one. He was still going to take good care of Lexi—he would just be doing it somewhere else. There was no reason to cause her unnecessary worry, knowing how important this retreat was to her.

''We're going to leave her a note at the house,'' he said, pleased that he'd thought of it. ''Just in case she gets home before we do.'' She'd appreciate that, he thought. It was an off chance that it would happen, but if it did, she would know where they were. She wouldn't be worried.

Drew promised herself she wouldn't be worried if they weren't there. She had gone through a few gyrations to get to a phone, but it would be worth it to hear Lexi's voice—and Whit's, she thought. She missed them, both of them. Eagerly she dialed the castle, smiling as the call went through.

When no one answered, her smile faded for a moment before it came back stronger. She was disappointed that they weren't there, but her trust in Whit was strong. It felt good. He had been so sure about taking care of Lexi. And he had pulled her around the corner for a goodbye kiss that was the kiss of a man who was confident he could give her what she wanted, too. She put her fingers to her lips, remembering it.

She hung up the phone. In a way she was glad they weren't just sitting inside the castle on this gorgeous October Saturday. She smiled to herself. No doubt they were off on some little adventure, which Lexi would tell her all about when she got home.

"We're approaching the city, Your Highness," the pilot announced.

"Which of us highnesses do you think he meant?" Lexi whispered to Whit as she looked eagerly out the window. Whit snapped his briefcase shut and watched her, smiling. All of the things that had become mundane in his life were an adventure now, with Lexi. She had explored his private jet from nose to tail, her stuffed animals in tow. And she asked him a thousand and one questions during the approach to the airport.

She held on to her crown while they landed, then obediently let go in order to hold Whit's hand as he whisked her off into a waiting limo. He didn't want anyone seeing her and asking questions. That's why they took the service elevator to the penthouse suite when they got to the hotel.

Lexi stood staring out of each window in turn, until she had gone full circle. Then she combed the rooms, while Whit finished last-minute preparations for his meeting.

When he came to a sticky point in international law, he called his friend Prince Lucas of the Constellation Isles, a longtime ally of Isle Anders.

Lucas confirmed Whit's interpretation.

"Thanks. I just wanted to make sure there won't be a hitch in this."

"You're sounding good," Lucas observed.

"Yeah. I'm feeling good," Whit said. He was, too. Just the thought of winning Drew and Lexi for good gave him confidence to burn. "How are things with you?"

"Same as before," Lucas said briefly.

After the unexpected death of his father the year before, Lucas had been given temporary rule of his country—but he could only claim the crown that was his birthright if he married by the end of the year, and time was running out.

Whit felt for him, but he knew Lucas wouldn't appreciate a pity party, so he said jokingly, "Still having trouble finding a willing woman?"

"Having trouble finding the *right* woman. You're the problem solver. Got any bright ideas?"

Whit was about to admit he didn't, when something occurred to him. "Actually, I just might have an ace in the hole for you, friend," he mused. "But you'd have to take a leap of faith."

"Just what have you got up your sleeve, Anders?"

"Not what. Who."

Lucas snorted. "If you're thinking about passing me one of your leftovers, forget it," he said, then added, "Not that I would expect anything as mundane as a fix up from you."

"Smart man," Whit said, grinning. There was a knock at the door. Room service, no doubt, with the supper he'd ordered for Lexi and himself. "Look, I've got to go now," he told Lucas. "I'll call you after this thing is signed, sealed and delivered. Till then, don't go getting married or anything."

"If the past ten months are any indication, there doesn't seem to be much danger of that," Lucas said dryly. Then he added seriously, "Good luck on the treaty, Whit."

By the time they finished supper, it was getting late. Whit asked Lexi to go into her bedroom to change.

A few minutes later she came back out again. "I'm ready, Prince Whit," she announced.

He looked up from his paperwork and found a surprise waiting for him. Lexi was dressed in the gaudy pink dress that she had worn in the play. Her hair had been gathered into a ponytail at the top of her head, pulled through the construction paper and glitter crown that she also wore. On her feet were her sparkly plastic beach sandals, and she carried a little vinyl purse in her hand. She beamed at Whit and curtsied.

He stared at her. "Lexi, why aren't you wearing your nightgown?"

She stared back at him. "My nightgown? Why would I wear that?"

"Because it's your bedtime."

"But," Lexi began, her lower lip quivering. "But I thought you had a meeting. And you would take me with you."

He dropped to his knees next to her. Apparently he hadn't taken enough time to explain things to her. "I do have a meeting," he said gently. "But I'm having it here, sweetheart. So we don't have to go anywhere."

"Oh," she said, plainly disappointed at not being able to strut her princess stuff in the Big Apple. Then she thought for a moment. "Does that mean people are coming here?"

He nodded.

"Famous people?"

Not to a six-year-old, he thought. But they'd probably end up with their pictures in the paper, if they pulled this off. "Sort of," he answered truthfully.

"I see," she said gravely. "We'll be entertaining here, then." She plunked herself down on the middle of the sofa. "When do our guests arrive?"

Whit stood up and reached his hand down to her. "After you go to bed, princess."

She stood up. "Bed? You mean, you're not letting me stay out here for the meeting?"

He led her back into the bedroom. "That's right," he said.

"Why not?" she asked, her lower lip trembling.

"Because you don't belong in this meeting," he said, searching her overnight bag.

"But I'm a princess!" she wailed, dissolving into tears.

"Princess or not, you're a little girl," he stated. He found her nightgown and tossed it onto the bed. "And it's your bedtime."

"But we're in New York!" she said, still crying.

"It's the same time in New York as home in Maine," he told her. "Bedtime."

That's when Lexi pulled out the heaviest ammunition of all. "If you were my prince," she said in a small, trembling voice, "you would let me stay up and be at the meeting."

She had forced his hand. *If he were her prince.* Ever since he'd found her note, that was what he had been trying to be; but Whit found that at the moment of truth, the right choice was crystal clear.

"No more excuses, Lexi," he said firmly. "Into your nightgown and into bed you go, so I can tuck you in."

She stuck out her lower lip. "I can tuck myself in," she said with dignity, wiping away her tears with the back of her hand.

"All right," he said reluctantly. "Then how about a good-night kiss?"

"No."

Whit felt deflated. He hesitated at the door. "I'll be right outside if you need me," he said softly.

Lexi turned her back on him and looked out the window. "I won't," she said.

It was late that night before Drew had another chance to use the phone. Lexi would no doubt be asleep, so Whit would know she was calling just to talk to him; but she didn't care. She did want to talk to him, to hear his voice. And maybe there in the dark, over the phone line, he would put into words what she had seen in his eyes and felt in his kiss. The words she had waited a lifetime to hear. Then maybe she'd have the nerve to admit that she had fallen in love with him all over again.

But just as before, ring after ring at the castle went unanswered. And so did the doubts that were beginning to rise inside of her.

By the wee hours of the morning, tempers were running short around the negotiating table in the penthouse suite. For one thing, Whit had insisted that the representatives of the two countries settle this thing before daybreak. He knew it could be done, and besides, he was bound and determined to get Lexi back to Anders Point by Sunday night. For another thing, he had banned smoking in the room—he didn't want his daughter breathing in any secondhand smoke— and the only thing both of the diplomats seemed disposed to agree upon was that smoking a fine cigar would make this unpleasant business more bearable. Whit's own temper was short because he felt like a dagger had been thrust into his heart, after what had happened with Lexi. He was beginning to feel like one of three ill-tempered lions in a very small cage.

A muffled cry came from the bedroom. Whit was up in a flash, grabbing for the doorknob. From behind him he heard one of the men grumble, "He's gone in there often enough tonight."

The other answered, "With a reputation like his, no doubt he's got a sweet young thing in there."

Whit would have smiled at how right—and wrong—the man was, if he wasn't so concerned about Lexi. The other times he'd gone in were just to look in on her, his heart heavy at her disappointment at bedtime. She had seemed fine, defiantly sleeping on top of the covers, still in her princess clothes. He wondered what was wrong now.

As he closed the door behind him, she gave another cry, but this time he heard what she said. "Daddy!"

It was as if the dagger that had been buried inside him all night was slowly being turned. He walked over to the bed. She was asleep, tossing and mumbling incoherently, but a moment later she said it again, more urgently. "Daddy!"

He sat down on the bed next to her, murmuring softly and stroking her hair. It was the first time his little girl had ever called him Daddy, a moment he had been looking forward to more than he'd realized, but it was bittersweet. Maybe she hadn't been calling him at all. Certainly she wasn't awake and wouldn't remember this in the morning.

Whit sat and soothed her. At his touch, or the sound of his voice, she settled down. As if his presence had been a magic balm, she dropped quickly back into what looked like a deep, untroubled sleep. He leaned down and kissed her on the top of the head, then stood in the darkness watching her and listening to her rhythmic breathing, before leaving the room.

He closed the door behind him and leaned back against it, taking a deep breath and vowing to himself that someday Lexi would call him Daddy for real. Being her daddy was worth waiting for, worth fighting for. Lexi was worth fighting for, and so were all the other children in the world. All the children in the two countries whose futures hung in the balance that night. By all that was sacred, he wasn't going to let them destroy each other.

The two men at the table looked at him expectantly.

Whit strode over to them. "Gentlemen," he said, "we are going to try a new strategy." He took a deck of cards out of his briefcase and slapped it onto the table. They both looked at him in surprise.

"The game is five-card stud," he said. "Winner gets what he wants on that sticking point in the treaty."

After a long silence one of them spoke. "What if you win?" he asked.

Whit carefully kept his lips from twitching. *If* he won? "Then I will dictate the terms of a compromise, which you will accept," he said. "Are we in agreement?"

They both stared at him. "Obviously you two are having trouble deciding who's going to shuffle and who's going to cut the deck before I deal. While you're doing that, I'm going to order us some refreshments." Whit deliberately turned his back to them while he dialed the phone.

"Hello, room service? I'd like a pitcher of cold milk and three glasses sent up to the penthouse. And some cookies along with that, too." He paused. "Milk, yes. No, not skim. The full-octane stuff. And cookies. No, not *biscotte. Cookies.* That's right, and lots of them. Either chocolate chip or those black ones with the cream in the middle. And make sure the glasses are wide, because we have every intention of dunking."

When he turned back around, they were still staring at him. Then one of the men picked up the deck and started to shuffle the cards. The other watched intently, waiting to cut the deck. With a lazy grin Whit picked out a cigar from the case one of them had put on the table and stuck it in the corner of his mouth. For luck.

Chapter Ten

By the time she returned to Anders Point on Sunday afternoon, Drew was standing on the verge of panic, with all ten toes hanging over the edge. After an almost sleepless night, she'd been relieved that the retreat had ended sooner than expected, giving her an earlier start home. But her relief had waned with each mile she drove and been replaced by fear as each stop at a phone booth had yielded nothing more than a familiar series of rings that hadn't ended until she'd hung up.

She drove by her house first and just slowed down enough to see a couple of newspapers piled in front of the door. There was no use wasting time stopping—Lexi and Whit obviously weren't there. She sped up the castle road and parked in front. The gates were locked, but she knew a way through the iron fence. It was no use. Banging on every door, ringing every bell, shouting at every window brought no response. There was no one there.

At last the solid ground she had been clinging to gave way, and panic swallowed her up. She might be a sheriff, but she was a woman first and a mother. Gruesome mental images of car wrecks, catastrophic illnesses and freak accidents plagued her, the only way her mind could explain their complete disappearance. Fighting down nausea, she made herself look over the edge of the castle bluff to the jagged and unforgiving rocks below, but saw nothing. Steeling her nerves, she decided she had better go back behind her house and do the same.

When she found nothing there, either, she decided to go inside to call for help. She started to throw the newspapers out of her way so she could open the door. On impulse, she opened up that day's.

Leafing past the national and international news, she got a chill when she saw something that caught her eye. It was a photo of Whit, safe and sound, getting off a plane. The brief caption simply raised speculation as to why he was in New York for the second time in a week. Nothing terrible had happened to him. He had simply left. Again.

New York! How *could* he? And if Whit was in New York, where in the world was Lexi?

She looked at the photo again, and this time saw something that had escaped her notice at first glance. Behind Whit's body was a little arm, raised as if to wave. Then Drew looked lower and saw a small pair of very familiar sneakers. Her mouth dropped open. It was Lexi, all but hidden behind Whit.

Her anguish increased. Not only had he left her again, he had taken Lexi with him this time. She stood on her porch, feeling betrayed, powerless and more alone than ever before.

Drew was still standing on her porch, leaning against one of the posts, when the limo pulled into the driveway. Looking up, she threw aside the paper she'd been holding and ran over to the limo. When she yanked open the back door, Lexi came tumbling out into her arms.

"Mommy," she sobbed, clinging to her and crying. "Mommy."

Whit was surprised to see Drew home early, but he wasn't surprised at Lexi's reaction, after what had happened the night before. Her anger had dissolved during the night, but she hadn't awakened her usual cheerful self, either. She had been quiet and pensive during the trip home, and Whit had left her to her thoughts, though he couldn't imagine what they were.

His own were crystal clear, even though it had been nearly dawn when the negotiations had finally come to a successful close. He finally felt like a father, a good one. He had done his best, and he was sure Drew would be pleased. He had been with Lexi every minute and taken good care of her. He had proven worthy of the trust Drew had placed in him. And that, he hoped, would make him worthy of her love.

Drew would agree with him about disappointing Lexi last night, too. He remembered her saying once that the hardest thing you had to do as a parent was to let your child fight her own battles—and face disappointment—while being there to lend support. The full meaning of this was clear to Whit now.

He was no longer Lexi's "prince." But that didn't matter. He only wanted to be her father.

Emotion welled up in him as he watched his daughter hugging her mother. He got out of the limo but stood aside, respecting their right to be alone together. He could wait for the moment when he and Drew could have their own private reunion; the one that, he hoped, would lead to their public union. It couldn't happen soon enough, as far as he was concerned. As soon as they could find someone to ask them to repeat the vows that were spoken in her office the other day.

But when Drew looked over at him, he was shocked to see that her face was as tearstained as Lexi's, and white with anger. She picked Lexi up and started for the house, but then stopped and looked back at him.

"How could you do this, Whit?" she asked, her voice shaking with suppressed rage. "How could you *do* this?"

"But Drew—" he started to explain, taking a step toward her.

"Leave...us...alone," she warned tightly, cradling Lexi against her protectively.

He reeled backward, then watched aghast as she marched into the house, leaving him with the awful finality of the sound of the slamming door.

Whit walked into the castle, alone but for the sting of Drew's words and the raw pain of his disbelief.

He had tried his best, but still he had failed. As a prince he had failed Lexi; as a father he had failed Drew.

The thing was, he knew that if he had to do it all

over again, he would do it the same way. It had felt right to him. He couldn't do any better.

He hadn't forgotten the promise he'd made to Drew, the night he'd first arrived at the Point. He had told her that if it ever came to what was best for Lexi, she had absolute say. Well, she'd had her say, and the message he had gotten was clear. If his best wasn't good enough, then he could never be the man Drew needed, for her or for Lexi. He couldn't change who he was.

There was only one thing for him to do now. He had had his chance, and given it his best shot. Now he would be man enough to step aside. He fished his suitcases out of the closet.

The phone rang. King Ivar's voice boomed over the line. "I found out why you finally stopped asking me for an assignment. You found one on your own, I hear."

Whit had known that word of the treaty would spread quickly, now that it had been signed. After he'd won the card game, both negotiators had accepted the terms of his compromise, which they both admitted was a fair one and one neither had thought of. "I did what needed doing," he said simply.

The king seemed taken aback at hearing his words of advice to his son. "I'm proud of you, Whit," he said gruffly. "Looks like you've found your own way at last."

Whit rubbed his hand over the back of his neck. "That's why you always gave me those different assignments, isn't it?"

"Yes. You had to find out for yourself that you

didn't have to follow in your brother's footsteps. His path was the wrong one for you.''

"You knew I would fail when I took over his revenue job.''

"I knew it wasn't the place for your talents,'' the king admitted. "But I didn't know what was, either. Only you could determine that, and you have.'' His voice filled with pride. "My son, a peacemaker. A noble role, and a fitting way to use your many gifts.''

His father's words reached across the ocean to fill a corner inside Whit that had been empty for a long time. Now that he was a father, he understood his own better. "It couldn't have been easy for you, to stand back and watch me struggle,'' he said.

The king was silent for a moment. "I see now that I could have been more supportive,'' he said at last. "I never did have your mother's warmth. But believe me when I tell you that all I ever wanted was for you to be happy.''

Whit squeezed his eyes shut, but didn't say anything.

"Where will you go from here?'' the king asked.

"I'll talk to you about that when I get there.''

"Here? You're coming back to Isle Anders?''

"Yes.''

That gave the king pause. "Son, have you finished all your business there?'' he asked slowly. "Have you done all that needed doing?''

Whit knew then that his father had known more than he had realized, when he had sent him to Anders Point. King Ivar had met Lexi at Erik and Julie's wedding. No doubt he had put two and two together and figured the whole thing out. But even if he did know who Lexi's father was, Whit couldn't discuss it with him. He had promised Drew to keep it a secret, and he would keep that promise. Especially now that he was leaving them, for good.

"Yes," Whit answered. "I'm all finished here. I'm packing right now."

King Ivar's voice rose. "And if I ordered you to stay?"

"I would leave, anyway."

"But, my son, you have never before disobeyed a direct order," the king said, astonished.

"I know," Whit told him evenly. "But a man has to do what he thinks is right." Even if he ended up disappointing someone he loved.

There was a heavy silence. "If you are doing what you think is right, my son," the king said at last, "then that is enough for me."

Whit hung up the phone wishing that had been enough for Drew, too. He was gratified that his princely role was resolved at last. But he knew that wouldn't ease his inner restlessness. Drew and Lexi held the keys to his heart; without them, any chance he had at true happiness, true love, true fulfillment, would forever be locked out of his life.

Drew helped Lexi unpack—every one of her fancy dress-up dresses, which just confirmed the fact that Whit had let her play the princess in New York. Lexi told her about flying on his private jet and staying in the penthouse suite, but she seemed preoccupied. After a while Drew left her and went downstairs to get her own bag.

As she was walking through the kitchen, she saw

a piece of paper on the counter. Reading it, Drew leaned against the counter, gradually overcome by regret. It was a note Whit had left for her to let her know he was taking Lexi to New York with him, along with complete information on where they would be staying and when they would be back.

She squeezed her eyes shut. If only she had remained calm enough to have looked for it *before!* The note just underscored the fact that Lexi had been perfectly safe the whole time—and Drew should have known that perfectly well, knowing how Whit felt about her. But her maternal fear that her daughter might be in danger had sent her over the edge, and she had reacted to that fear with anger.

Maybe there was more to her fear than that, though. She had been afraid of losing something ever since Whit had come back; not so much of losing Lexi to him, but of losing control of the way she had held their lives together all this time. Of losing her heart yet again to the man she loved. Most of all, of losing her dream forever.

She heard Lexi call her, so she went back upstairs. Lexi was sitting by her window, which looked out toward the castle. "Mommy, I need to tell you something important," she said.

"What is it?"

"It's about Prince Whit. He passed the test."

Of course. The prince test. "When he took you away to New York?"

Lexi nodded.

"And you flew on his jet and stayed in a fancy hotel room. I'll bet he treated you like a princess."

"Oh, no, Mommy," Lexi said, shaking her head.

"You don't understand. He wouldn't let me have any fun at all. He wouldn't let anyone see me with him, and I had to eat all my vegetables. We didn't go anywhere, and he wouldn't let me come to his meeting. I even had to go to bed at *bedtime*."

Drew began to realize that she *hadn't* understood at all.

"And I was mad, and I said some mean things to him," Lexi went on. "And I told him he wasn't my prince after all."

"But you said he passed the test."

"He did."

And then Drew remembered what Lexi had really been looking for.

"I know he just has to be my daddy. My *real* daddy," Lexi said. She looked up at Drew earnestly. "He is, isn't he, Mommy?"

Tears spilled over onto Drew's cheeks. Every life had its moment of truth, and this was hers. "Yes," she said in a choked voice. "He really, really is." Whit had nothing left to prove, to her or to anyone. Lexi's search was ended, and she would never find a better father. Whit had been a good father to her since the day he'd found out that he *was* her father. He might not ever be conventional, but convention wasn't all it was cracked up to be, anyway, Drew thought, smiling through her tears. He loved Lexi dearly, and that love shone through in all he did for and with her. That was all that mattered.

"I knew it," Lexi said, satisfied with herself. "But now there's one thing left to do. I have to break the spell, so that he can be my daddy again. Only I don't know how to. Do you, Mommy?"

Drew looked down at her daughter, her beautiful, bright, imaginative, starry-eyed daughter. They had their hearts set on a fairy tale, she and Lexi, and all the wishing in the world wouldn't make it come true. But something else could.

"Do you know, Mommy?" Lexi repeated.

Well, Drew knew one thing, at last. True love *was* enough. It had always been enough, and it always would be. Whit was the man for her, just as much as he was the father for Lexi, and true love would overcome any obstacles that stood in the way of that dream coming true.

"Why don't we walk up to the castle and see him?" Drew suggested.

Lexi looked out the window. "I think we better run. His car is parked out front, and the trunk is open." She turned to Drew with a worried look. "You don't think he's leaving, do you? Remember, he said he always *has*."

Drew remembered, all right. But this time she had a feeling he wasn't leaving by choice. She was afraid he was being driven away by the things she had said and done in anger, and even more afraid that it might be too late to take them back.

They raced up the castle road and knocked on the front door. When there was no answer, Drew pushed it open.

Whit was throwing the last of his things into his suitcase, trying not to give way to misery, when he heard a noise downstairs.

"Daddy!"

He froze. It sounded like Lexi's voice. He thought

he must be dreaming, the way she'd been last night when she'd said that.

She called out again, louder this time. "Daddy!"

Then he heard Drew. "Whit, where are you?" she said, her voice echoing through the stone corridors.

Now he knew he wasn't dreaming. Lexi was calling him Daddy, and Drew was letting her. Whit felt as if he had been hit blindside. He couldn't find his voice to answer them.

Lexi raced up the big stone staircase, with Drew right behind her. They both came to a stop in Whit's doorway, when they saw he was packing.

"Oh, Mommy," Lexi said, her voice breaking. "We're too late! He's *leaving!*"

Holding her close, Drew spoke to Lexi reassuringly, but she was looking right at Whit. He felt his heart pounding erratically. "Even if your daddy has to leave for a while, he will come back."

"Al-always?" Lexi asked, fighting back sobs.

"Always," Drew said firmly. If she said it out loud, it would come true. It had to. She swallowed, meeting the scrutiny of his blue eyes.

"How d-do you know?"

"Because we love him. This is where he belongs."

Her saying it made it true. Without a word Whit walked over and put his arms around them both. The woman who was the love of his life. The little girl who was his own daughter. They were his family now, and he embraced both the responsibility and the joy they would bring to his life.

Lexi wiggled down from their arms and started dancing around the room. "Mommy! We broke the spell!"

Whit pulled Drew flush against him and kissed her, hard. "What spell?" he asked.

"It's a long story. Tell you later," she said, and kissed him back, harder.

Lexi stood still and stared at them, giggling. "You two look funny," she said. "Are you going to get married?"

"Yes," Whit said when he came up for air.

"When?"

"Just a minute, I'll ask your mother," he said, and kissed Drew again.

Lexi laughed so hard she collapsed onto the bed. When Whit and Drew toppled down next to her, she popped up again.

"Are you two going to be doing that for a while?" she asked. When neither of them stopped kissing to answer, she announced, "Then I'm going to go play."

When he realized they were alone, Whit broke off the kiss to look at Drew. "There's another reason I won't be leaving," he said huskily.

"What's that?"

"I love you."

She had felt his love before, but this was the first time she had heard it. "Say it again," she said in a choked whisper.

He looked her right in the eye. "I love you, I love you, I love you," he said, and reached up to wipe a tear from her cheek. "Sweetheart, I've spent seven miserable years learning that you can't run away from love like ours. I intend to spend the rest of my life right here by your side, reveling in it. And..."

"And what?"

"And being the best father I can be to our wonderful child."

She smiled at him through her tears. It was all she'd ever dreamed of. But that didn't mean she couldn't have a new dream. "Any chance you'd want to make that plural?" she asked.

Children? He hadn't thought about that, but why not? "I'm open for negotiation on that point," he said cautiously.

"Then let the negotiations begin," she said, giving him a kiss that made him decide it might be nice to prolong the negotiations for a while—maybe a year or so. As for now, somewhere in the back of his mind, Whit thought hazily that it was a good thing that Lexi was nearby and awake. Otherwise he might be tempted to do things with his fiancée that were best left for the wedding night. As it was, they found enough to do to keep them busy for some time, while the sounds of Lexi playing drifted up from downstairs.

It was almost time for supper when he and Drew wandered down, arm in arm, and found Lexi playing in the ballroom.

He smiled proudly. With that imagination of hers, his daughter was never lacking for things to do. His daughter. Suddenly he couldn't wait to call his father and brother and tell them the news.

"What'cha doing, princess?" he asked her.

"Don't call me princess," she growled at him.

"Why not?" Drew asked, hardly believing what she was hearing.

Lexi galloped up and stood in front of them, hands on hips. "Because I'm not a princess, I reckon."

Drew smiled at her. "No, honey. You are. You *really* are."

"You're my daughter," Whit explained, unable to keep the pride out of his voice as he said the words out loud at last. "That makes you a princess."

"I'm not a princess and don't call me one," Lexi warned with an exaggerated sneer. "Or you'll be buzzard bait." She aimed her forefingers at them, thumbs pointing to the ballroom ceiling.

Whit gave Drew a puzzled look, which she answered with a shrug. He looked down at Lexi again. "If you're not a princess, then what are you?" he asked.

"I'm the roughest, toughest cowpoke in these parts," Lexi said, in her best Western drawl. She put her fingers back into the invisible holsters on her hips. "You can call me 'pardner' from now on. See you around the corral." And with that she started galloping around the ballroom again.

Drew laughed out loud. "Are you sure you're ready for fatherhood, pardner?" she asked Whit.

To her surprise he answered, "No." Then he looked her up and down, slowly, and lowered his voice a sexy notch. "I think I'd better practice being a husband for a while first, Sheriff. I'm thinking about a quick wedding and a long, long honeymoon."

Drew swallowed. "Suits me fine," she said, a little breathlessly. "But what about the little varmint yonder?"

"Aw, I don't reckon she'll mind taking her cowpoke act on the road for a while," Whit drawled. "There's a grandfather, an uncle and an aunt in Isle

Anders who'd be tickled pink to ride herd over her while you and I take a trip around the world.''

''Wow,'' Drew said. ''Were you thinking about a boat or a plane?''

He gave her a sexy grin. ''I was thinking about a bedroom, honey,'' he murmured. And after his next kiss, so was she.

* * * * *

If you liked THE PRINCE'S BABY, don't miss the exciting conclusion of Lisa Kaye Laurel's series, ROYAL WEDDINGS.
Coming in 1998!
Only from Silhouette Romance.

ELIZABETH AUGUST

Continues the twelve-book series—36 HOURS—in November 1997 with Book Five

CINDERELLA STORY

Life was hardly a fairy tale for Nina Lindstrom. Out of work and with an ailing child, the struggling single mom was running low on hope. Then Alex Bennett solved her problems with one convenient proposal: marriage. And though he had made no promises beyond financial security, Nina couldn't help but feel that with a little love, happily-ever-afters really could come true!

For Alex and Nina and *all* the residents of Grand Springs, Colorado, the storm-induced blackout was just the beginning of 36 Hours that changed *everything!* You won't want to miss a single book.

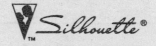

36HRS5

Take 4 bestselling love stories FREE

Plus get a FREE surprise gift!

As seen on TV!
Free Gift Offer

With a Free Gift proof-of-purchase from any Silhouette® book, you can receive a beautiful cubic zirconia pendant.

This gorgeous marquise-shaped stone is a genuine cubic zirconia—accented by an 18" gold tone necklace.

(Approximate retail value $19.95)

Send for yours today...
compliments of ▼ Silhouette®

To receive your free gift, a cubic zirconia pendant, send us one original proof-of-purchase, photocopies not accepted, from the back of any Silhouette Romance™, Silhouette Desire®, Silhouette Special Edition®, Silhouette Intimate Moments® or Silhouette Yours Truly™ title available at your favorite retail outlet, together with the Free Gift Certificate, plus a check or money order for $1.65 U.S./$2.15 CAN. (do not send cash) to cover postage and handling, payable to Silhouette Free Gift Offer. We will send you the specified gift. Allow 6 to 8 weeks for delivery. Offer good until December 31, 1997, or while quantities last. Offer valid in the U.S. and Canada only.

Free Gift Certificate

Name: _____

Address: _____

City: _____ State/Province: _____ Zip/Postal Code: _____

Mail this certificate, one proof-of-purchase and a check or money order for postage and handling to: SILHOUETTE FREE GIFT OFFER 1997. In the U.S.: 3010 Walden Avenue, P.O. Box 9077, Buffalo NY 14269-9077. In Canada: P.O. Box 613, Fort Erie, Ontario L2Z 5X3.

FREE GIFT OFFER
084-KFD

ONE PROOF-OF-PURCHASE

To collect your fabulous FREE GIFT, a cubic zirconia pendant, you must include this original proof-of-purchase for each gift with the properly completed Free Gift Certificate.

084-KFDR

SILHOUETTE WOMEN KNOW ROMANCE WHEN THEY SEE IT.

And they'll see it on **ROMANCE CLASSICS**, the new 24-hour TV channel devoted to romantic movies and original programs like the special **Romantically Speaking—Harlequin™ Goes Prime Time.**

Romantically Speaking—Harlequin™ Goes Prime Time introduces you to many of your favorite romance authors in a program developed exclusively for Harlequin® and Silhouette® readers.

Watch for **Romantically Speaking—Harlequin™ Goes Prime Time** beginning in the summer of 1997.

If you're not receiving ROMANCE CLASSICS,
call your local cable operator or satellite provider and
ask for it today!

Escape to the network of your dreams.

See Ingrid Bergman and Gregory Peck in *Spellbound* **on Romance Classics.**

Daniel MacGregor is at it again...

New York Times bestselling author

NORA ROBERTS

introduces us to a new generation of MacGregors
as the lovable patriarch of the illustrious MacGregor
clan plays matchmaker again, this time to his three
gorgeous granddaughters in

THE MACGREGOR BRIDES

From Silhouette Books

Don't miss this brand-new continuation of Nora Roberts's
enormously popular *MacGregor* miniseries.

Available November 1997 at your favorite retail outlet.

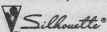